William Simpson

The Man From Mars

His morals, politics and religion

William Simpson

The Man From Mars
His morals, politics and religion

ISBN/EAN: 9783337068653

Printed in Europe, USA, Canada, Australia, Japan

Cover: Foto ©Andreas Hilbeck / pixelio.de

More available books at **www.hansebooks.com**

THE

MAN FROM MARS.

HIS MORALS,

POLITICS AND RELIGION.

BY

THOMAS BLOT.

―――――

SAN FRANCISCO:
BACON & COMPANY, PRINTERS.
1891.

INTRODUCTORY.

My habitation is upon the plateau of a mountain in California. I entered this region and became a settler by a fortuituous event. About thirty-five years ago, I took a summer outing from a close application to business in the metropolis, and came here for a deer hunt. One of those beautiful animals that I had wounded with my rifle led me further into this wild and picturesque locality than I had intended to go, and I thus arrived upon this spot, as I believe, the first white man that ever sat foot upon it. Reaching here late in the afternoon, I found myself too far out of my path to return by daylight, and so, building a fire, I spent my first night alone in this weird place. It was the first time in my life that I had slept where some human creature was not within the sound of my voice, and from that night I date a change of sentiment, thought, and feeling, which has altered my career, and made me, what I have chosen to be, a recluse.

I had been living in the world about thirty years amid the artificial surroundings of a city. I had scarcely looked upon the sky and heavens, except between the margins of opposite house-tops. I had

viewed from infancy, without emotion, the rising
and setting of the sun from a horizon of chimneys
and steeples ; and when these exhibitions first presented themselves to me here in this crystal atmosphere, with an expanse from this altitude so new
to me, they appeared like a revelation. I seemed
to have been suddenly ushered into the world, and
to be looking for the first time in my life upon the
stupendous phenomena about me.

Until this moment I had not approached a reali-
zation of the magnificence and prodigious wonders
which the heavens afford to our observation. It
was here also that I began for the first time to enjoy those beautiful and curious processes of nature,
where the bursting germs, ascending gradually out
of the soil, change their shapes, multiply their organs, and after a time crown themselves with bril-
liant and deliciously flavored flowers. In my new
observation and intimacy with plant growth, with
some previous knowledge of the science appertaining to it, and with a newly discovered delight in
marking the changes of position and the characters
of the heavenly bodies by the greedy acquirement
of all the information within my reach, I have come
to forego, without regrets, the social pleasures of
life.

By the liberal laws of my country, I have become
possessed of this attractive spot, and thus far, I have

chosen to retain it in its natural state. I came here a young man. I am now old. Thirty-five years of my life have been spent on this elevation, with a self-banishment from society, without in the least abating my interest in human affairs. My communication with the world is mostly through books. A weekly newspaper or two, and such other publications as I may order, are left for me in a hollow tree several miles away by the district messenger; and thus no important event or new discovery in the world escapes me.

I have constructed with my own hands a cabin, having much convenience and comfort, and also some outhouses, which shelter my poultry and a pair of gentle cows, which latter, finding abundant food in the natural grasses about, come to me regularly at milking time, seemingly as much for the pleasure of being caressed, as to furnish me the principal nourishment of my life.

There is a trout stream in the center of my posession, with expansions here and there, which serve as bathing places for myself, and out of which pure and cool drink is supplied to the few domestic animals about me. This stream makes its way through the bottom of a hollow, and is so overhung by the lofty branches of trees which grow upon its borders that the sunlight only enters in patches, and is so reflected by the restless surface of the water as to

mark its devious way with the appearance of a line
of flashing mirrors. The surrounding dense body
of foliage, from at least a hundred varieties of trees
and shrubs, is tinted with a variegation of color seldom seen outside the tropics. This charming spot
has its voices, as restless as the lights and shadows
which play about within. Each miniature waterfall
has its liquid note ; while during certain hours there
comes from every quarter of the foliage above a
confused melody of birds, who, I have reason to believe, assemble there for entertainment and gossip.

Outside of this watered region, my homestead is
interspersed with openings, where the rich loam
only awaits the labor of cultivation to produce a
wealth of grain or fruit. Every tree and shrub within my possession of a half a mile square, by long
familiarity, seems to have become a part of myself.
We are living and ageing together. I have watched
in them the development of infancy, the slow and
gradual approach to youth, and the turning point
from maturity to old age. Among these old mon-
archs of the woods is here and there one tipped with
the signs of superannuated decay. About their feet
lay many of their withered, sapless limbs. They
have lost their symmetry, and stand in scraggy outline. I see from year to year their gradual giving
up of life, while beside them a new generation
arises. There is a fellow feeling between us. My

hair grows thin and white, and my step is no longer firm and elastic. Like them my share of life is growing to a close, and yet I am an infant in years compared to many of them. I bow to them with a sentiment of reverence. They are my old men. The younger ones are my children — mine! What a grand thing it is to have these in my possession, — to hold in my own right such a choice piece of this blossoming earth, where all the mysterious forces are at work day and night for me alone!

I have come also to have an abiding interest in the creatures who by nature are inhabitants of this place. Long ago have I laid aside my gun as an instrument of destruction, and it rests now on its pegs above my pillow only as a defense. By slow degrees I have gained a confidence with the native birds and animals which surround me, so that it is wonderful how many of them welcome me and enjoy my presence. There swarm to my poultry fold at feeding time myriads of quail and other birds, who, with an amusing assurance, run about my feet and dispute for the crumbs that I scatter. The gray squirrels may be often seen scampering down from their hiding places in the trees to meet me, in expectation of their accustomed relish of wheat grains, which are stowed away for them in my pockets. I have three pet deer, quite tame and domesticated, whose intimate acquaintance was brought about in a singular way. Sitting

on my doorstep one bright afternoon, I had listened
for some time to the baying of hounds in the neighboring mountains, when presently there came bound-
ing toward me, in terror, a trembling doe, and with
her beaming eyes fixed upon me, seeming to invoke
my pity, she literally threw herself into my arms.
Taking in the situation at a glance, I tried to force
her into my door before the dogs arrived. Too late
for that, I could only arm myself with a stick from
my woodpile, when the whole yelping pack were
upon us. It was a hard fight, and only after many
bites and scratches from the disappointed hounds
did I beat them off. I kept her in a secure outhouse
for a few days, where two beautiful fawns were born
to her ; and ever since the mother and offspring have
been my favorite pets, following me about like children. My acquaintance with other of the creatures
about, though not so intimate, is still of such a confidential kind that they manifest no terror at my approach, and I am thus enabled to realize, by this free
exhibition of them, how teeming with animal life is
the earth in its most favored parts.

In my earlier years I have felt the cold blasts and
torrid heats of other climes. I now rest myself in
the happy satisfaction that I have found in this equa-
ble temperature and agreeable surroundings a place
where one may look upon life as a blessing. I have
acquired enough knowledge of some of the sciences

to make an instrument or two of service to me, and I take especial interest in my telescope of three inches aperture, in the use of which I spend many an hour which otherwise might hang heavily on my hands. I have also a good microscope and field glass. Through the latter I bring to view the distant hillsides and mountain tops, observing, frequently, groups of deer grazing tranquilly, and at times a family of panthers gamboling on the green carpet of an opening, or an eagle feeding her young upon the inaccessible brink of a precipice; and on rarer occasions, a bear complacently munching acorns under some prolific old oak a mile away. My microscope has revealed to me a world of wonders. I have discovered by it the limitable range of our senses, and how far below as well as above us the infinite extends. I grope about in the darkness of my understanding between an atom and the outside limit of the stars, every step toward either showing an increase of distance. These things I pursue, not with the spirit and application of a student, but rather for the entertainment which they furnish and the meditation they invoke. I have learned all that is known of the motions and eccentricities of heavenly bodies within my telescopic vision, and I never look upon them without rapture. What are all other shows to this? How many of these countless worlds are inhabited? What beings are upon them? How do

they compare with us? Has it been given to them
to comprehend eternity? Is knowledge with them
intuitive or acquired? Thus do I lose myself in
these bewildering fancies.

It may appear that I have avoided my share in the
cares and duties of human association. If I have,
it is from no lack of sympathy with my kind. I look
upon my fellow-men from my distant and somewhat
isolated point of view, without the usual diversion
of active affairs, and both my pity and admiration
are aroused. The sufferings and sorrows of my kind
seem appalling to me from this position, while their
heroism in the struggle for knowledge seems to me
grand beyond expression. I feel myself in the midst
of civilization, and yet apart from it. If I have been
a loser from that lack of social attrition which arous-
es the activities of thought, it is, nevertheless, certain that I have not been submitted to a combination
of those influences which render an error plausible.
The opinions and thoughts of the world come to me,
and I pass them in review with a full sense of the
fallibility of individual opinion, as well as an abiding
faith in the steady approach of that collective truth
which, sooner or later, will overspread the world.

THE MAN FROM MARS.

CHAPTER I.

My telescope is mounted in an apartment adjoining my cabin, with an elevated exposure, and has some extra contrivances for the convenience of adjustment, designed and constructed by myself. The instrument can be raised and lowered at pleasure, and is protected by a movable dome, which is easily laid aside by means of a couple of pulleys. It is a good one, and for its size has remarkable power. I have been enabled to reach with it double stars of the sixth magnitude, frequently observing even Orion, with its beautiful double and multiplied systems. I can easily discover with it the most distant planet Neptune, and by their progressive displacement, I have seen and recognized with it most of the asteroids. I can get with it a fine view of Jupiter, that magnificent planet fourteen hundred times larger than our Earth, and have observed the black spots upon its surface, and the transit of its moons. The grand spectacle of Saturn and its rings is brought to my observation with remarkable clearness. I have so frequently looked into the dismal

caverns and upon the towering mountains of our
satellite, the Moon, that its marks and bounds are
as familiar to me as the neighboring hills.   But life
is short, and amid all this illimitable sea of worlds,
I have fixed my attention upon but one, for that
special study which my few remaining years will
permit.   The heavenly body which most engages
my attention is, excepting our satellite, the nearest
one to us, our neighboring planet Mars.

I believe that body to be inhabited by beings in
many respects like those of the Earth.   My conclu-
sion is adduced from many known facts concerning
it.   Mars has an atmosphere like ours.   Its density
does not differ materially from the Earth.   The heat
it derives from the sun, possibly modified by atmospheric conditions, is quite likely the same as ours.
It has zones of varying temperature, and seasons of
summer and winter like the Earth.   Its days are
about the same length as ours.   The ice and snow
of its polar regions are plainly perceptible, and vary
in areas exactly in accordance with its changing
positions and distances from the sun.   From which
we may infer, without a doubt, that its atmosphere
contains moisture of the same chemical composition
as ours, and is condensed into rain and snow as with
us.

There are striking points of difference, however,
between Mars and the Earth.   Its diameter is a lit-

tle less than half that of our planet, and its surface is only about a quarter of ours, while its volume is but a seventh part of our globe. Furthermore, instead of a single satellite like ours it has two moons, which revolve in opposite directions around it, neither of which in point of size can be compared to ours.

My knowledge of astronomy not being profound, it has been the greatest pleasure and gratification to me to verify, by my own observations, the calculations and theories of the abler scientists. Appertaining to Mars, it is perhaps needless to say that there is a diversity of opinion among astronomers touching its physical conditions. The unusual red color of its reflected light, its bright and dark spots, and the variation. which is observed in the forms overspreading its disc, are differently accounted for. It is among such questions as these, then, that my imagination and ingenuity are free to exercise themselves, and the desire to settle some of these disputed points to my own satisfaction increases the eagerness of my observation.

I have watched for many years, with anticipations of pleasure, when Mars would be in opposition,—or in other words, when, during its revolution upon its orbit, it comes nearest to the Earth. These occurrences of about every two years are holidays of pleasure and enjoyment to me. There are, however, rarer oppositions of Mars, which occur only twice in a century, when the distance between us is reduced to the smallest limit ; and it has been my good fortune to get a finer view of this heavenly body at this shorter distance than will any human being at present alive.

It can well be imagined what a supremely interesting event this was to me. Days before its culmination did I watch its progress approaching nearer and nearer the Earth. Each succeeding night exhibited to me its slowly magnifying proportions, and the greater distinctness of objects on its surface. Here was a world of beings, no doubt, with aims and enterprises like ours, rolling headlong through the heavens with a known velocity of fifty-four thousand miles an hour. This planet was now approaching, hourly, its greatest possible proximity to the Earth. That I should lose no time in devouring, as I may say, this unusual spectacle, I had provided my telescope with a kind of clockwork contrivance, by which it exactly kept pace with Mars on its westward course. During these few days, I had forgotten everything else in my eagerness to feast my eyes on this rare show. The nights had been favorable to observation ; and each evening after turning my instrument on the rapidly approaching planet, my interest became so transfixed and absorbed that all my ordinary physical wants were suppressed. I had lost in these few days of mental excitement all inclination for food and sleep. No one could be freer from superstition than I, yet my mind was uneasy under an unaccountable premonition. It gave me some anxiety to think that on the very night of culmination, when my interest would be at its height, a change of weather might cut off the scene. But aside from this, in my somewhat feverish condition, I could not restrain a sense of some impending and momentous event in my personal affairs. Some strange influence seemed to be disturbing the usual tranquil and placid condition of my mind. I aroused myself from this, however, and became thoroughly myself when the sun went down on the evening of my hope, and left an atmosphere that was as perfect as I could wish for. The sky was calm and clear, with just enough moisture in the air to increase its transparency. The ordinary evening sounds appeared stilled. Neither nighthawk nor owl seemed abroad, and the usual rustling of leaves and swaying of tree-tops was suppressed by a calm that struck me as strange. The day had been moderately warm, and the sun-distilled odors of the firs and pines, condensed by the coolness of twilight, were filling the air with an agreeable perfume, as though Nature was burning incense in the celebration of some ancient rite, during which every living and breathing thing about seemed bowed in silent reverence. I had never known until now what assurance there was in the natural sounds which nightly fell upon my ears. In my mountain home no feeling of loneliness ever came over me before. I felt an especial longing now for the sound of a human voice, for a companion upon whom I might discharge myself of the suggestions and beliefs appertaining to the subject of my investigation and study. My mind was filled with conclusions touching the physical condition of Mars, which each new observation tended to corroborate. I had my theory to give of its rose-colored light. I had seen the clouds moving upon its surface, its polar snows, and its very atmosphere. I had no doubt whatever, now, that it was inhabited, and the anticipation of soon seeing it in its most favorable opposition with the Earth, was accompanied with a yearning that some human creature might share with me the rare spectacle.

As the twilight faded, I looked with my naked eyes toward the east, and my other world was showing its red light near the horizon like a rising sun in miniature. At midnight it would reach its culmination, when viewing it through the least possible thickness of our atmosphere in its vertical position, I would see it as no human being could see it again for over half a century. The oppressive silence and tranquility remained unbroken, and as I seated myself in my observatory and adjusted the telescope, I felt myself not quite in my accustomed vigor of health. The temperature had perceptibly raised, when it had usually fallen as the night advanced. The air was sultry. A sensation of qualmishness came over me. It came to my mind now that I had abused myself by a long neglect of sleep and regular meals. But no sooner had I brought my instrument to a focus than I was myself again. Our beautiful neighbor was mounting the heavens, reflecting the sun's light in a delicate crimson tint, and in size of outline beyond my expectation. I could plainly mark its rotation upon its axis by noting the slow movements of spots upon its disc, and their sudden disappearance over its limb. The hours seemed minutes to me. My fatigue and illness were forgotten. In my rapture of enjoyment the lingering wish increased that some fellow creature might share it with me. My telescope, in tracing the planet's course, had very nearly obtained a vertical position, when I was astonished to see the distant world suddenly disappear, and begin to vibrate back and forth over the aperture of my instrument. A moment's reflection explained the matter. The Earth had shaken. So trifling, however, was the disturbance about me that it had not been felt. But I had lost my focus, and Mars was already on its backward journey. My grand holiday was over.

I immediately lowered the telescope and replaced

its protecting dome.   Gathering the few hasty notes
I had prepared during my observation, for future
reference and elaboration, I made my way to an
apartment of my cabin which serves me for a library
and bed chamber.   A number of shelves filled with
books occupy one of its sides.   My bed rests in a corner. An easy chair stands beside a table in the center,
and under a window, proportionately large, fronting the south, is placed a cushioned lounge of some
pretensions to comfort and luxury.   I threw myself
upon this, after laying away my papers, and the
lower panes of my window being on a level with
my head, I looked out into the night.

The moon in its last quarter was just peeping
over a near mountain.   Its light, partly obstructed
by a network of tree-tops, was throwing figures of
light and shade over the adjacent opening, so that
the ground appeared to have spread upon it a col-
losal carpet, with fantistic decorations of ebony
and silver.   The air had grown a trifle cooler.   A
gentle breeze was stirring out of the West, and the
silence, that had recently fallen so mysteriously
upon me, was being followed now by a normal condition of unrest.   As the moon rose higher, its fanciful shadows upon the ground dissolved, and the
level plateau adjacent to my window was uniformly
covered with a clear, bright light.   Looking again,
and quite sensibly impressed with the changed con-

dition of things about me, I descried the figure of a man, not far from my window; and, strange to say, I was neither alarmed nor startled at his presence. His face, of which I saw but little more than its profile, was turned upward looking at the moon, and its expression was unmistakably one of admiration and wonder. His long, and apparently well-cared-for hair and beard, reflected a golden sheen under the light above. His arms were folded, and his shape and attitude impressed me as being majestic.

While fixing my gaze intently on this strange form, an expression of something wanting about it took possession of me, when presently I observed with surprise, that, although standing under the bright and unobstructed light of the moon, no shadow was visible about it. He remained for some time as immovable as a statue, gazing upon our satellite as one who had never before looked upon so wondrous a sight, and then, with the air of one on unfamiliar ground, he made an inquiring survey of my cabin, and then directed his careful footsteps toward my doorway.

CHAPTER II.

THIS strange figure entered my cabin, and without introduction or sign of salutation seated himself in my easy chair as though he were a member of my household, an apparent rudeness which will be explained as I proceed. I had now the first opportunity to get a good survey of my visitor. He was a person of surpassing loveliness. His face was of that spiritual kind which is seldom seen off the canvas of some of our art masters, and it reflected a kindness of heart that is never realized except by the purest religious fancy. His form was so high and elaborate in its development, that I have only seen an approach to it in the best models. His singular attractiveness I can only compare to that affinity which comes of pure sexual love, captivating the beholder with a presence which drives away all thought but it. His complexion had that ruddy clearness and transparency indicative of perfect health. The hair of his head and beard,—both long and waving over his shoulders and breast,—was of a hue that can be best described as the color of the ripe filbert, with the fineness and luster of unwoven silk. His hands, although scrupulously clean and finely shaped, bore the unmistakable signs of manual toil ; and yet he had the superior air and manner of one whose mission it was to instruct, As he sat before me I felt like a child in the presence of a loved and loving parent. My impression of him was entirely correct, since his first word of utterance to me was a term of endearment.

" My brother," said he, " you have a beautiful world. That moon of yours is magnificent."

To me this was a happy beginning. Here was, thought I, a man after my own heart, whose soul was above the common things of life. I could compare notes with him touching my study of Mars. Providence had then sent me, at last, what I had so wanted,—some one to share and enjoy with me the triumphs of my labor; so I immediately said to him : " As to the moon, it is certainly very serviceable as a night reflector of the sun's light ; but, since its size is comparatively insignificant, and its surface desolate and uninhabited, it is thus an object of very little importance among heavenly bodies. Speaking of magnificent planets, what do you think of Mars ? "

" Mars suits me," said my visitor.

Thinking my question too general, I inquired : " Do you think Mars inhabited? "

" I am a good proof that it is," said he. " I left that planet — let me see — by your time, about one hour ago."

"I either misunderstood you, or you are not serious. It is impossible."

"Ah, my brother," said he, "you are very little advanced in a knowledge of the properties of intelligence. I am here by a process as yet unknown to you, and which may be best described in your language as reflection. I am here by reflection. That is to say, my natural body is at my home, on the planet which you call Mars. Its spiritual counterpart is here. You have already an inkling of this strange faculty of transferring intelligence, in some of the phenomena on which is founded your spiritualistic creed. We, of the planet Mars, have been in the enjoyment of this discovery for centuries; and while you of the Earth are only able by your appliances of science to measure the size of our planet, compute its distance, estimate the shape and extent of its orbit, and indulge in some vague conjectures appertaining to its condition, we have been making a close and interesting study of your social affairs, including, of course, your morals, politics and religion. You have only measured us as a planet. We have measured you as a people, and at least one of us, as you perceive, has mastered your language. Besides, our development is over ten thousand years ahead of yours. We can tell you more of your history than you know yourselves. At a period of yours described by your writers as the stone age, we had converted electricity into a motor and illuminating agent. I know your thoughts. You are surprised at what I have said, and wish me to tell you something of the planet upon which I reside.

"It will interest you to know that about the equatorial regions of Mars is found its highest civilization and densest settlement. Your torrid zone, and the corresponding section of our planet, are widely different. In ours, the climate is delightfully and evenly temperate. The extent of our surface, as you know, is very much less than yours, but the uniform quality of our land for cultivation, and the smaller water surface, compared with yours, supports a population whose numbers would astonish you. You may as well discharge your mind of the many conjectures which ascribe to each planet a quality of matter and intelligence peculiar to itself. The whole universe is a unit, as your spectroscope, and the bodies from space that fall from time to time upon your surface, must have suggested to you. Variable states of density and temperature modify the forms and organs of animal and vegetable life, but matter is everywhere the same.

"Your chemists have just arrived at that point of knowledge where ours were forty centuries ago. Yours recognize over sixty forms of matter as simple and elementary, while ours have reduced them all to one,—the unit out of which all creation is formed. From this you may infer that our discovery of the compound nature of the metals enables us to make them at pleasure. This was a most fortunate and timely knowledge for us, since they are distributed very sparsely on our planet. It will no doubt be a strange thing to tell you, that we make gold at a less cost than iron, and that consequently it is the cheapest metal in use. You are about to ask me whether we make diamonds. We have made them for centuries. Our factories turn them out in masses for the ornamental parts of buildings, for which they are remarkably adapted on account of their brilliancy and indestructibility."

My strange visitor rested a little here, with the evident intention of reading my thoughts, and of enjoying my surprise. While I was marvelling what great things chemical science must have done in other ways, he appeared to anticipate my question.

"My brother," said he, "we are indebted to the science of chemistry for more than I can readily enumerate. With us, as with you, a large number of common and abundant substances differ only a trifle in chemical composition from others which are in great demand for the purposes of life. The science of chemistry enables us to convert one into the other at will. Thus, from wood we manufacture sugar, starch, and any number of other useful com-

modities.   By the double decomposition of air and
water we generate a heat which, for economy and
easy regulation, is better than anything the universe affords.   The clumsy, unclean and inconven-
ient use of wood and coal for fuel is with us a practice of the past."

"You have," I ventured to enquire, "railroads
and boats for transportation ? "

"We have neither," answered my visitor, "nor
do we require them, for reasons easily explained.
There are two conditions of our planet which render the navigation of the air entirely safe and successful.   They are the greater density of our atmosphere, and the diminished force of gravity compared
with yours.   Our air ships, as you would call them,
are easily made to sustain and move large cargoes,
by vacuum chambers and electric motors.   Our in-
ventors have long since surmounted the difficulties
of adverse wind currents, and these vessels, of both
public and private use, may be seen constantly moving about in all directions, and at all altitudes, with
but few serious accidents.

"There are no large oceans like yours on Mars,
and our rivers are so small as not to serve the purposes of commerce.   You will perceive, then, that
our facilities for navigating the air were bestowed
upon us as a means of transportation, in lieu of the
convenient waterways which you enjoy.   As you

may anticipate, from the small size of our rivers, there are no extensive mountainous water sheds upon our surface. Instead of your immense, desolate, and storm-beaten seas, we have a series of lakes, everywhere varying in size, but none of them larger than seventy-five of your miles long, and forty broad.

" The relative density between water and an animal body being such on our planet as to render the possibility of drowning by accident impossible, the fear and horror existing with you of involuntary immersion in the depths is entirely unknown. Our numerous lakes are therefore scenes of the most enjoyable, and what would be with you reckless, diversion. The upsetting of a boat with its load of excursionists, no matter where, results in merely a harmless frolic. The human body there sinks in the water only a little above its middle, and we have contrived, by web-like fastenings to the hands and feet, a means of propulsion so rapid as to nearly equal our speediest locomotion on the land. During our long summers, when the temperature of the water is agreeable, lake journeys, especially by the young, are among our most popular amusements. This, to you, strange condition of density is productive of a state of affairs partaking of the humorous, although leading to much domestic perplexity and annoyance. Our children take to the water in the

summer season as naturally as your water fowl, and
the loss of offspring upon the lakes, at that tender
age which precludes their knowledge of the return
direction, is the source of an immense amount of
parental disturbance and worry. The straying of
children upon the waters is attended, however, with
but little danger ; since, if by any possibility they
remain undiscovered during the night, they can,
owing to the buoyancy of their bodies, sleep tranquilly and delightfully upon their backs, resting
upon the soft cushion of the waters until rescued,
as they are sure to be on the succeeding day, by
one of the numerous air ships constantly skimming
the surface.

"Our land is generally rolling, and there is a constant water movement in the channels connecting
these small bodies of water, not in a uniform direction toward the sea, as with you, but in all directions, thus saving to us a power for mechanical purposes than which nothing better can be conceived.

"Our cities, as you may imagine, are not located
as yours are ; but, since one place is as good as another for a distributing point, the rule has been to
build them up where all conditions were favorable,
chiefly considered of which have been the health,
comfort, and pleasure of their inhabitants. It would
be doing us injustice to believe that, with our long
period of development and progress, we have not

achieved something far ahead of you in the sanitary and labor-saving appliances about us, especially in our metropolitan districts. In the first place, we use no woods whatever in the construction of our buildings, having discovered long ago a tendency during its slow decay to absorb and retain the germs of disease and uncleanliness. Neither is its durability satisfactory; and its ready inflammability and lack of strength render it unfitted for our purposes. We use, instead, a metallic alloy unknown to you, which is susceptible of a high polish, as inoxidizable as gold, and with that character of penetrability which permits fastening with nails and shaping by tools, with even greater exactness than you work with wood.

"Our cities are all built with uniformity. Their growth is invariably from the center outward. Their location is not a matter of chance, as yours generally is. No site is chosen without the thorough examination and approval of a sanitary commission, whose knowledge and sincerity we respect. Their foundation is made by the laying out of a large circular enclosure for the location of all public buildings, among which, in the center and more magnificent than all in its imposing loftiness and artistic finish, is our temple of worship. From this center radiate a set of wide and uniform thoroughfares, and these are crossed at regular intervals by circular ones, which begin at the center and are repeated to the circumference as a series of concentric rings."

The man from Mars became silent for a moment, and I observed that for the first time his face was clouded a little. He had spoken of a temple of worship, and it had started in my mind a wish to hear something of the society and morals of his people, and how they compared with us ; so I said to him : "I am grateful for your kindness in describing some of the material surroundings of your people, but I would like very much to know something of your inner lives, of your thoughts and beliefs, and how they affect your social condition."

"My brother," said he, "you wish me to make a comparison between our society and yours. I can scarcely do so without the risk of giving you pain. With our greater advancement, we look back upon you as travelers over the same rough paths. Your journey is even a more difficult one than ours. In your present state, you appear to us as a world of discord, confusion, and strife. While we were long ago resolved into a single, homogeneous people, you are still divided into nations and countries, unridden yet of the barbarous pride of combat. We have but one religion. Yours are many and antagonistic. I shall briefly make for you the comparison you wish, hoping that it may bring no sense of pain to you, for, to speak the truth, the cruelty, the intense individual selfishness, and the strange superstitions of the inhabitants of the Earth will pass away out of the ages to come.''

CHAPTER III.

"Comparing your society with ours," began my celestial visitor, "is like describing the difference between your present intellectual condition, and the state you were in during your cave-dwelling period. In our review of your progress, we recognize two chief agencies at work which have regenerated us, viz : the steady growth of human sympathy, and the fading out of old superstitions. In our advanced development, with the first of these, we have achieved a state of things in our society quite likely beyond your hopes. For instance, that feeling of regard and affinity for each other which is seldom found among you, except in the midst of family ties, we hold one for another among all. If I were to select from among you a domestic circle, the most refined and correct, its disturbance and anxiety from the sorrows and misfortunes of one of its members would scarcely represent the feeling in a body of our people for the misfortunes of any. We are shocked at your cruel indifference to the feelings of one another. When we see one of you sinking by the wayside, by means of one of the evils which you naturally inherit ; or overwhelmed, perhaps, with the penalties of a misadventure, and looked upon by his fellows regardless of his smitten condition, we can find no parallel to it among ourselves, except in the traditions that have come to us out of our remote ages.

"Your national antagonisms, your cruel wars, and the immense sums wasted by you in maintaining millions of your people, trained for the sole purpose of slaughtering their fellows, we regard as the one most disgraceful relic of your former supremely barbarous state. While, by the process of social development, all your most cruel brutalisms have disappeared within the range of your higher civilization, the remaining one, of sending masses of your people into deadly combat for the settlement of political and religious questions, is retained for reasons which are not wholly in concurrence with our sense of right. In the first place, no element of justice enters into the arbitration of a question, whose settlement rests entirely upon the physical strength of the contestants; and all international settlements by this means are but temporary, when the winning party has not coincidentally a prevailing sense of justice in its favor. All your wars and battles, without a result on the side of equity and truth, have been fought in vain. Your bloody misjudgments of one century often are, and are ever like to be, reviewed and resubmitted to the same sanguinary and delusive arbitration in a succeeding one.

In these brutal encounters you stain your hands
and garments in the blood of your fellow men without remorse, because the wild instincts of your
nature have never been suppressed in that particular
direction. Those of you in authority, both civil and
religious, have this to answer for. For the sake of
a concurrence in the selfish scheme of your rulers,
they have instituted a series of glittering rewards
for the most skillful of their wholesale murderers,
and you have in that way been educated to honor
most, those who could deal the heaviest blows.

"We cannot take a survey of the motives which
have instituted nearly all these sanguinary and
dreadful encounters among you, without a sense of
horror. Your civilization has witnessed only a
single one of these terrible conflicts, wherein a
purely humane question was involved. Your religions have not only been used to sanction this dire
carnage, but have even themselves been participants
in the slaughter of millions of your people. You
are not yet freed from the savagery of your remote
fathers, who, ages ago, entered those fierce contests
between tribe and tribe, with strong personal interests in the outcome. The loss or gain of a battle
meant to them either a share of spoils or probable
torture and death. Yet you have kept alive this
inclination to collective combat, when individual
loss or gain seldom cuts any figure in the incentive

2

which impels you to battle.   And even beyond these
physical encounters, your struggles of life appear,
from our point of view, to be divided between defense and attack, like the beasts of prey which still
linger on your borders.

"Your society presents to us the spectacle of a
continuous skirmish among yourselves, your whole
mass struggling to mount the summit of their individual hopes and ambitions, wounding and bruising
each other with cruel unconcern.   Our experience
has taught us that this unhappy social condition is
entirely due to the crude and imperfect stage of your
development.   Each of your new epochs brings
some approach toward a better terrestrial life; but
you have not fairly considered nor endeavored to
surmount the chief obstacle to your progress in that
direction.   You have not yet learned to deal justly
with one another.   By your system of unequal advantages, one class is permitted, and even encouraged, to prey upon another one.   One or more of
you will enter upon a scheme of personal gain without the slightest concern for its effect upon others.
You have permitted, from time to time, the passage
of laws having a direct and unmistakable tendency
to throw your wealth into the hands of the few, and
as a consequence, to increase the hardships of the
many.   Your generation exults over all preceding
ones in its progress in science and knowledge; but

even that has not served to soften or remove the as-
perities of your lives, for the reason that most of the
available material of this new advance has been
prostituted to serve the interests of the few.

"The growth of your social betterment rests almost
entirely upon the total of your disciplined thought,
yet by your methods, correct thinking is the rarest
thing among you. Your social field, instead of
being evenly stirred and seeded, is cultivated in
spots and patches. Even your knowledge has been
converted into a weapon of tyranny and oppression,
and it is oftener pursued in the love of self than for
the benefit of kind. Out of the helplessness of your
neglected and unfavored masses, come the greater
number of your individual accumulations of wealth.

" In our stage of progress such a state of things is
impossible. The performance of an act inflicting
injury or even discomfort upon one or more fellow
beings in our society, brings its punishment in the
general condemnation and disgrace which follows.
Active benevolence, which is with you an impulse,
sporadic and exceptional, is with us an ever-present
emotion, and upon it we have founded the chief
pleasures of life. We have no eleemosynary establishments, because they are not needed. There can
be no suffering from destitution among us, since each
person finds in his own surroundings the ready,
helping hand. No neglected orphan wanders about

uncared-for, because each family finds its pleasures increased by the opportunity to bestow shelter. Every dwelling is open to all, and no assuring salutation is needed to welcome the visitor. He enters the house of the stranger, as the stranger would enter his, by the right of the universal brotherhood which prevails.

"The love of our kind forms the corner stone of our single religion, just as the like is made the foundation upon which your many creeds are built. But while your religious teachings have brought no great fruits, ours have yielded a harvest of glorious consequences. If it will interest you, I shall tell you why."

CHAPTER IV.

AT the dawn of, and during the first stages of their civilization, the people of the Earth found themselves surrounded with natural forces which, in their scant knowledge of the laws of the universe, were ascribed to the arbitrary and willful caprices of a great hidden being. They found a mysterious power above them, and everywhere an overwhelming evidence of design. The unthinkable and unknowable character of the infinite and eternal was not then acknowledged ; and the failure of any to explain this unseen intelligence and power incited their imaginations to do for them what the closest investigation had failed to accomplish. As may have been expected, they clothed their imaginary deity with the qualities, propensities, and passions of themselves. Any violent convulsion of nature was taken by them as a certain sign of his anger; while the normal state of rest, and the undisturbed processes of animal and vegetable development and growth were looked upon as concessions in their special favor. From a belief in the supervision of the deity over every single one of the innumerable processes of nature, they naturally imbibed the idea that they each were objects of his personal watch-

fulness and attention, and as a consequence, that all
the fortunes and vicissitudes of their lives were dependent upon his moods. It may very well be supposed that with this conception of the deity, the
chief purpose of life would be to find favor with
Him, to discover his wishes, and to learn his commands ; since, in accordance with this simple and
crude idea, every one's success and comfort in life
depended upon his conciliation. With these views
of nature and the universe, they came in due time
to observe that within themselves were feelings
and sentiments entirely apart from the ordinary
epicurean impulses which governed them. We may
imagine in those cruel times the warrior standing
over his prostrate victim with upraised club, stayed
in the act of killing him by a sentiment of pity, and
enjoying afterward as a result of his compassion a
pleasure which was as strange and unaccountable
to him as his first sight of a comet. There was no.
apparent motive whatever for his humane act. On
the contrary, it had deprived him of spoil, and reduced the honor of his victory. And so, all the inclinations to virtue which brought no material and
immediate rewards were regarded as mysterious and
inexplicable as the great hidden power, and by a
very natural sequence of reasoning, a part of it.

As your civilization advanced, it was to be seen
that the virtues, and especially those which had a

direct influence upon material welfare, grew and enlarged. The path to honor was no longer exclusively through carnage and victory, and the possession and cultivation of certain virtues brought consideration and respect. It was at this critical stage of your progress that there was inflicted upon you an evil greater than any your people have known. You were not content with viewing the deity as we do from afar, and with accepting the impulses of virtue as a part of yourselves, instituted for the wise purpose of a continuous self-development toward a better earthly life ; but instead, in your unreasonable yearning to communicate with the supreme Author, you surrendered yourself to the wiles of the seers, and became the willing dupes of their delusions.

There is nothing more unhappy to tell of you than the consequences of this grave error. Your assumed possession of the commands and wishes of the deity in the shape of a revelation, has proved more a misfortune than a blessing to you. In the first place, it has lowered your conception of the deity below ours. It has turned your religion into a contest. It has rendered possible the establishment of certain ecclesiastical bodies among you, who, while assuming entire control of the morals of your people, are beset in their internal parts with all the vices which come from cruelty, cupidity, and love

of power. Besides, your formulated conditions of
punishments and rewards have degraded religion
from a cultivation of virtue for itself, and the immediate good it brings, to a selfish scramble, each
one struggling to shoulder his way into the most of
celestial delights.

It can be easily understood why your religion,
with all its crudities and superstitions, has taken so
firm a hold upon your society. You are constituted
as we are, with the same inherent elements of progress. The steady increase of your affinity for the
virtues, and those who practice them, is a marked
quality of your career, and as they all lead, in one
way or another, towards that union of interests
which constitutes the perfect social state, you are
thereby impelled by a natural and providential desire
to build them up. So that, as a matter of fact, there
being an inherent love of goodness ingrafted in
your very natures, your religious creeds have attracted you to them, and held you in fetters, under
the false theory that the good within you is but a
contribution from their exclusive and abundant
sources of supply.

It has been your misfortune to be held captive
throughout your progress by the shrewd designs of
your seers and prophets, who have not failed until
recently to supply you with an occasional change of

supernatural pabulum, to meet the new wants of a steadily advancing development.

When at a certain stage of your civilization, about two thousand years ago, you had attained a point of intellectual culture among the few, the fruits of which have been reflected upon you to this day, in some of the grandest recorded achievements of human thought, and while the masses were left to take their undirected way among the empty superstitious which conceded nothing to the growing human sympathy, a seer appeared among you, who served rather as a suggestion than as an immediate success. After the lapse of sufficient time from his death to allow full scope for romance, there was built up out of his memory by your seers a picture of all the virtues which had been growing within your hearts, so entirely adapted to the new age that all the pent-up forces of human sympathy within its scope and influence surrendered to it. But what might have been a triumph and a boon to you in the new impetus to a better and broader humanity, unfortunately held concealed within itself the subtle machinery of your seers and prophets, and was guarded by their evil eyes, so that with this tremendous lever to move you in the direction of their purposes, instead of advancing you, they have turned your civilization back upon itself more than a thousand years. No historical fact is more capable of demonstration than this.

None has been more persistently and ingeniously denied, and no natural sequence ever followed more directly a moving cause. From a free and independent exercise of the intellectual activities in the direction of science, art, philosophy, and all knowledge pertaining to yourselves, the Earth upon which you dwell, and the universe, so far as your vision extends, the whole current of your thoughts was turned by the new doctrines toward a paradise, compared with which all things of the Earth were trifles. When you were brought by the fascination of these promises, and the unflagging efforts of an interested body of ecclesiastics, to a general belief in these doctrines, you sank into an intellectual torpor, from which you only emerged by a protest of your reason not yet wholly suppressed.

You cannot fail to see the utterly dehumanizing tendency of the influences which surrounded you for so many centuries. The common aims and purposes of your lives were submerged by the one engrossing wish to reach heaven; and while your imagination was carried away by its picture, you were led, without hesitation, to place your feet upon the neck of any earthly enterprise that seemed to stand in its way.

From the beginning of your history you have accepted one object of worship after another, each one an ideal impersonation of the goodness which was

inseparably a part of yourselves, and which was given
to you for the wise purpose of making your society
possible, and to perfect it; just as the parental instinct was bestowed upon you to protect your infants.
All these subjects of adoration have perfectly reflected your intellectual condition, and have been discard-
ed, one after another, as they outlived their uses ;
until you are just now beginning to realize, that for
all these many centuries you have been virtually
worshipping yourselves. Your present ideal will, in
time, share the fate of those which preceded it, and
in the absence of a prevailing superstition, your
seers luckily cannot build up for you another one.
Your long period devoted to the pursuit of phantoms
is rapidly passing away, and your new age of ration-
alism is approaching. You have no just conception
of the evils it will remove, and the glories it has in
store for you.

The difference between your present and future
religion can be easily outlined. Your present religion, from a long course of erroneous teaching, is intense, aggressive and hysterical. It feeds and fattens
itself upon the miseries of life, which it does not undertake to remove, except in a meretricious way for
effect. Your religion of the future will be tranquil
and voluntary, and its chief mission will be to permanently reduce the evils and misfortunes of life to
a minimum. The impulses of your present religion

are entirely apart from the moral sense, a significant
fact easily substantiated by a glance over the every-
day life of your people.   Except in their observance
of religious forms, your devout are not distinguished
from your profane.   The practical virtues are no
greater among believers than among unbelievers.
Your coming religion will be founded upon the moral
sense, and will be inseparable from it.   It will support no doctrine of a ready and convenient atonement
for bad acts, as the present one does.   It will teach
you that there can be no complete reparation of an
evil deed except its undoing, and that such an act,
once performed, spreads its dire consequences in accordance with its enormity over a part or the whole
career of the doer.   It will not undertake to un-
burden the conscience of a crime, nor to give assurance of celestial bliss to the most heinous of offend-
ers, upon the trifling and fallacious compliance with
religious forms.

Your peculiar religious beliefs have so shaped and
moulded your character that we have observed, what
you are not likely to see of yourselves, certain traits
or inclinations which are not promising as factors in
your ultimate regeneration.   Your churches, with
the shrewd purpose of rendering their services invaluable, have given you to believe that your natural
tendencies are evil, and that the unavoidable misfortunes and sorrows of your lives are but penalties

for your many misdeeds. The general acceptance
of this belief has lowered your pride, and given you,
to some extent, that character of dejection and sub-
missiveness which is entirely subversive to the attainment of any destiny to be reached by yourselves.

There is a quality of mind which we acknowledge
as, above all others, the one which has assisted us to
our present very desirable social condition, and that
is the feeling to resist the perpetration of a mean or
bad act, on account of the sense of degradation it inflicts upon the feelings of the doer. This motive of
conscience, so plainly the offspring of self-esteem,
and growing out of a cultivation of the mind alone,
without any regard whatever to creed influences or
teachings, is totally ignored, either as a promoter
of virtue or preventive of vice, by all the religions
that have existed upon your planet. The reason for
this is easily explained. Under the knowledge that
a cultivation of the mind and conscience, without
creed influence, was capable of doing for you a better service in the advancement of your morals than
your churches have performed, it has been made a
part of their doctrine to belittle and abuse your
purely intellectual faculties, under the unwarranted
and unreasonable imputation that the free exercise
of your reason was an assumption beyond your
right. And all this, too, in face of the overwhelming evidence about you, that the most corroding

and dangerous of your vices germinate and seed themselves only in places where the mind lies in fallow.

There comes to us from our remote ages, through tradition and history, an account of some superstitious beliefs, but it has been our good fortuue never to have had them built up into a system so overbearing and harmful as yours have been. It cannot be said of us that we ever denounced honest intellectual efforts in any direction as a crime; and your punishment of such, with all its atrocious details, serves as a lesson for the whole universe of worlds never to put trust in the smooth tongues and insinuating ways of the seers, for the truth is not in them.

I hope you will not infer from what I have said that the people of Mars have not great reverence and veneration for the Deity. Indeed, it is the universal belief among us, that the animus which is within us to do good to ourselves, and to make pleasant the ways of life among each other, is but the prompting of that divine presence which is leading us aright in the direction of the still better things to come. As we see in all living things a constant development upward toward a state of perfection, and having, of all creatures else, that within us most susceptible and easy of advancement in the universal march, we simply take our place in the line. What we have accomplished in that direction in our government, society, and morals, gives us new heart to further efforts, and if our methods may be of any service to you, I will give you some further account of them.

CHAPTER V.

THE people of Mars are impressed with the belief
that the governments of the Earth have made no
great advance in the benefits and usefulness of their
legislation during the last two thousand years. We
recognize amongst you, only as movements of progress, some provision, particularly in your own
country, for the free education of the people, a few
sanitary attentions, and a slight awakening to
the interests of your labor class, as about all worth
mentioning. It is true that your governments, after
originating themselves with only the simplest duties,
have come in time, as your civilization advanced, to
take on increased and complicated services. But in
the multiplication of their duties, there is unfortunately little to be seen but an extension, in various
directions, of their first purposes ; which may be
briefly stated as a defence of assault from without,
and a protection of person and property within. We
have come to regard the obligations of government
as something much beyond these, and this difference
of view affords a marked instance of our development and advance.

Our idea of life is, that since it is all we are given
to know from the first to the last stages of our con-

sciousness, it is our duty and privilege to improve
it, and enjoy it to the fullest innocent and rational
extent ; and that to this end there can be no separation of the moral and material interests ; for it is but
an honest acknowledgment to say, that constituted
as we all are, the crown of contentment and happiness is only for him who successfully cultivates both.
Under this belief, the general supervision of both
moral and material affairs is placed in the hands of
our government. Church and State are therefore one
with us, and it is entirely due to the rationalistic
character of our religion that the alliance has proved
so conducive to our progress and happiness. There
can be no such peaceable and continuous union with
you at present, because from the nature of your
religious doctrines there must be a conflict of authority ; but you will come to it in time, as out of it,
more than all else,— as I will endeavor to show,—
will come the fullness of your destiny.

Your efforts for the suppression of vice and crime,
since the first stages of your history, are futile to a
degree that must be appalling to you, and the cause
of your failure is due to conditions plainly apparent
to us. These conditions are that your governments,
for all these centuries, have taken no official cogni-
zance of virtue, and have failed to see that there
existed in their patronage of good deeds that tangible
reward which would place all ambition for honor and

prominence among them on uncompromising terms
with evil. You have only attempted to suppress
crime by punishment, while the powerful stimulus
to virtue which your governments afford of precept
and example have been neglected. Although, in
your undeveloped state of greed and selfishness, you
find it unsafe to trust your material interests in the
hands of those irresponsible bodies which you call
monopolies, yet you bestow the whole keeping and
guidance of your morals upon societies and organizations of your fellow men, who are even less responsible to authority than they. Under this state of
things, how can you expect anything better than
your present chaotic state of religion, and the loose,
unguided, unrewarded, and wholly spontaneous
morality of your people ?

Our government, in the furtherance of its religious
duties, has for centuries made a special recognition
of the virtues, and particularly those which bestow
good upon others, and it is only by the practice of
such that public honors are achieved. One of the
happiest consequences of this has been, to elevate
only the most exemplary of our people to the head
of public affairs, and from this comes a confidence
and regard between our representatives and people,
which you can scarcely appreciate after your experience. Goodness therefore, as we understand it, is
the only path to honor, and the necessary high

character of all holders of public trust reflects a
distinction greater than those of any other positions
in life. . This in turn, as you may readily perceive,
induces a spirit of emulation to reach such elevated
places, beyond all considerations of emolument.

As a part of our moral system, we hold the education of our people to be an indispensible and necessary adjunct. In that we go a great deal further
than what appear to us your narrow and mercenary
views. In a representative government like your
own, you have been constrained to adopt a system
of free education, for the purpose of securing the
safety and permanence of your institutions ; and
with no other motive even, it is surprising that you
will be divided in opinion touching the extent to
which learning may be profitably imparted for this
end alone ; because, to us it seems that when you
have conveyed to your youth no more than the elementary branches of learning, you have provided
but little else than a convenience to them in the
business affairs of life. It is only when the higher
branches are acquired that the government receives
an equivalent for its outlay, in the well-disciplined
and safe citizen returned to it.

We have, however, motives beyond all this in the
education of our masses, and chief among them is the
purpose to furnish knowledge to the minds of all, out
of which good may be naturally evolved ; and thus

you will see at once how learning has become the chief part of our religion. You are slow to acknowledge the great value of your purely secular education as a moral agent, because of its disturbance recently with your cherished traditions ; but this reason, great as it is, is supplemented with another one, which fully accounts for the earnest opposition of your ecclesiastics. So long as the learning of your schools was mixed up with creed influence and teachings, it was virtually a part of the church, and in harmony with it, but on a separation of the two, they become enemies by a well known social law ; your churches with their awowed purpose of improving your morals, and your secular schools, while in the performance of their duties, occupying the same competing field.

You may easily imagine that, with the religious impulse added, we have carried our education a good deal further than you. We consider the proposition unjust, that learning should only be bestowed in accordance with the occupation or station in life. Your planet has always been beset with the evil of social classes, which only increases with the advance of your civilization. You can never rid yourselves of this fruitful source of disturbance except by our method, which, as a matter of public policy, pushes the education of every individual to the point of his capacity. In this way we have, completely obliterated the class interests and feelings. We have been enabled to do this under conditions which you do not at present possess. Instead of the military or martial spirit which prevails with you, and which is cultivated for purposes which appear to us unworthy of your age, we have generated among ourselves an ambition in the ways of knowledge which takes its place.

We have leaders and heroes as you have, but not one who has not gained his honors by some act in furtherance of the material, intellectual, or moral progress of his race. The memories of your greatest men are more honored by us than by yourselves. Men go down to their graves yearly among you whose achievements are the admiration and talk of our whole people. He of you who discovered the theory of planetary motion, he who found the law of gravitation, and he also who ascertained the principle of evolution in organic life, are scarcely known upon the Earth, except among the cultivated few; while the whole world of Mars is impressed with the services they have bestowed, and discuss the great and everlasting effects of their work.

We have found much in the path of science that would astonish you, and at each discovery the achievement was applauded and echoed from one side of our planet to the other. At each one of these advances we feel ourselves getting nearer to the

Deity. A triumph of science with us is a triumph of religion, and while we go on strengthening our-selves, and taking new heart at each step in the direc-tion of knowledge, a like progress with you only brings the superstitious framework upon which your religion is built into decay.

Our religious devotion is essentially buoyant, even joyous. The sorrows of life which are not the direct and indirect results of indiscretions, and violations of natural laws, we regard as an inheritance and not a punishment, and we endeavor in all conceivable ways to lighten them and make them easier to bear. For those in sickness among us, the hand of love and sympathy is never absent ; and among the firm and undisturbed convictions of philosophic thought, death is only a regret and never a terror. Your creeds administer to the final end in all ways to a point of agony ; they have ingeniously devised a theory of horrors for it, out of which has been made to come their chief sustenance and support. The path of life which they declare as the only one leading into the promised eternity of bliss, is the tortuous and diffi-cult footway winding like a maze among the shadows of their churches.

Although attentively guided throughout in this prescribed journey of life by your ecclesiastical teachers, and your entrance and exit made difficult without their help, yet, by the very nature of their

doctrines, they could only bestow upon you at the
last scene of all a torturing doubt. We have promoted the serenity of death by removing as far as
possible its sorrow. With us, the individual in his
last moments is not overcome with any sympathetic
dread of that approaching suffering for the wants of
life among dependents, which so often couples the
agony of separation with an overwhelming sense of
despair, as your society is constituted. The end
comes placidly to us, in the belief that as we came
from the Deity, so in the last we go back to Him;
that the life beyond must be a higher life, because
the moral sense grows constantly within us; and
that the region ahead of us must be a free, open,
and hospitable one, with no agonizing barriers sepa-
rating families and friends, because, in the growth of
our tenderness and attachment to each other, we can
safely predict the evolution of a better and happier
state.

Prayer, in the sense that it is understood and performed by you, we regard as worse than superstition. It is an outcome of your lowest stages of
mental evolution. It is the spirit of that willing
self-abasement and fear, which prostrates the savage
before his idol, soliciting aid in his works of carnage,
or immunity from some violated law of nature, or
safety from some convulsion of the air, land or sea.
Carried forward into your civilization, it has become

no less unreasonable. For thousands of years you
have been daily calling on the Deity for favors, not
one of which has been granted, except seemingly
by a coincidence. The most conclusive tests have
failed to convince the devout among you of the fal-
lacy of prayer, because, as an institution of your
churches, under their theory of atonement, it furnishes a ready escape to the conscience ; and for the
reason also that it affords to the imagination, in its
striking and novel situations of converse with the
author of worlds, a semblance of that pleasure which
the lowly feel for concessions from the great.

It is quite in keeping with your conceptions of the
Deity that you should grovel and debase yourselves
before Him. The whole tenor of your religious
thought has been made to take on this color of self-
degradation, which, while serving to throw you
more completely into the hands of your theological
superiors, is not warranted by any possible relations
with the being you address. You represent upon
the Earth, as we do on our planet, the very highest
form of life. We both are the triumphant outcome
of a process established by the great Author infinite ages ago. On us only, among all beings, has He
bestowed the wonderful attributes of thought and
reason, which make us a part of Himself. We are
the only inheritors, by his own beneficent act, of the
power to discover and to enjoy his beautiful meth-

ods of work, and those magical transformations of mind and matter which convert, out of the dead ashes of the past, the blooming present, with its assuring hope of a fruition to come.

What hint have we, therefore, in all his works, that He has created us otherwise than as a labor of love, and as the fullest expression of an evolutionary skill, which marks all things about us? By what authority, then, are you called to bow yourselves in constant self-abasement before your great Father, who, with parental solicitude, has thrown open the whole Earth for your household, has given you the power of domination over all creatures upon it, and has taught you to make playthings of the very elements which surround you? By what authority, except the unworthy example of your own barbarian instincts, which demand for place and power a homage, whose degree of prostration marks, with a singular exactness, your career all along, from the savage ruler to the cultivated monarch?

Outside of the fact that your continuous mendicancy has accomplished nothing for you, you have an abundance of negative evidence to hint that your incessant supplication, instead of bringing to you favors from the Deity, has shadowed upon you in an unmistakable manner the signs of his displeasure. For, as he has raised you gradually out of the lower forms, and enlarged your capacities, until in the last he has taken you into his confidence so far as to teach you the methods of his work, and to deliver up to you the hitherto pent-up forces for your convenience and use, yet in the progress of these concessions it is to be noted as a significant fact, that your prayers have served rather to obstruct than to promote them.   Indeed, as there is nothing so conclusively the evidence of divine presence and help as material and intellectual progress, it will be difficult to show, in the record of terrestrial things, that the supremacy of prayer has not invariably been followed by a temporary withdrawal of this divine assistance and support.

CHAPTER VI.

OUR veneration for the Deity, which is truer and more sincere than yours, arises from a widely different conception. Looking back upon the ages, and what they have brought to us, we perceive that each new development in matter brings an increase of those qualities which give us pleasure to behold. Beginning with the most unattractive shapes, this process of change in organization and symmetry, by an unalterable law of the Creator, brings to us out of the ugliness of the past the beautiful of the present. Since, therefore, we see Him constantly at work, transforming the ugly into the beautiful, we believe He is pleased with the colors, shapes, and qualities of things which delight our own cultivated senses. Acting then on this conviction, we surround ourselves with the beautiful in nature and art.

The change, in the form of matter, is not more instructive than the steady modification of intelligence, which, from its primitive ignorance, superstition, and brutality, has been gradually raised step by step to its present higher grade of thought and action. We recognize here a fact most important and significant to us. While the divine energy is steadily at work, couverting lower forms of matter into higher oues, we are given no part in the proceeding. It goes on without our assistance, and we have no power to diminish or accelerate its steady onward course. It is widely different with intelligence. That is given iuto our hands, with all its grand possibilities. In that, we have evidence of the divine confidence to promote its advance in view of the blessings it holds in store. Taking this view, we have for ceuturies cultivated the mind in all directions of knowledge and feeling, as the chief part of our religion. The motion of the spheres is not more certainly the work of this great being, than are these progressive changes in mind and matter.

We believe vice and ugliness to be convertible terms, the latter a quality due to imperfectly developed matter, and the first a property of intelligence in the same imperfect state ; just as beauty and virtue describe together, or separately, the same advanced evolution.

But while working in harmony with the Deity, and assisting in his purposes, we have constantly in view, as an incentive to action, the consummation or goal to which all these changes tend. We believe the outcome to be a spiritual life with all things knowable, and a state of perfection and happiness beyond our present conception. Happiuess, then, being a religious aspiration, we promote it in all ways to the innocent and reasonable inclinations of our present state.

Our religion is consequently more jubilant than solemn. We have no torments in store in it, nor long drawn agonies and mortifications of the flesh. Its only business with death is to smooth its pillow, and to reduce its attendant sorrows to the minimum. To the misfortunes of the present our religion extends its hand of sympathy and material help. To what purpose should it introduce and dwell upon the miseries and sorrows of the past? We let the dead ages rest. We can find nothing in their ashes to compare with the living. The present is better than the past, as the future will be better in exact measure with the new truths discovered, and the old fallacies cast aside. You rake among the emanations of an early and imperfect development for monitors and guides, and do honor to them for the mysteries they invoke. You place the withered hand of the mummy into the warm palm of the living, and your ceremony of introduction is a prayer that the living body may never depart from the dead form.

The untenable and unsupportable premises upon which your religions are based will lead to their decay. Nothing of them will remain to you but their spirituality. Shorn of their superstitions, and guided by the intellect, the spiritual part of them will be retained by you as a jewel repolished and in a new setting.

The orthodox among you are suspicious of the inroads of science, unaware of the fact that in due time it will fix upon your belief the conviction of a future spiritual existence without the shadow of a doubt. When you will have arrived at that point, your ways of morality and progress will be so much increased, that you will regard your previous advancement as trifling. To some, your science appears to lend encouragement to materialistic beliefs. This is only your half knowledge. For some time to come your discoveries will tend in that direction of thought, but all this will be superseded with a firm conviction of the existence of the Deity, and your steady approach to Him. The period of danger to you will arrive when you will have made the discovery, as we have centuries ago, of what may be described in your language as the universal diffusion of intelligence amongst all matter, inorganic as well as organic.

It may be a startling proposition to announce to you that the quality which gives you the power of abstract thought is possessed in a lower degree by, for instance, the stones which lie beneath your feet; yet such is the case, for we have demonstrated beyond a doubt that the chemical forces and affinities are nothing else but low, restricted, and insensible

forms of intelligent action. The fact is best shown
by the building up of organic bodies in their multiplication of cells. Eacn cell arranges itself in place,
and makes way to its successor, under an inherited
impulse of action from which it is unable to depart.
What are known among you as natural forces, are
merely forms of unconscious and restricted intelligences, which have only the power to act in limited
directions. They both build up matter and tear it
down for us. They shape the crystal with mathe-
matical uniformity, and mark out the form of the
plant with unerring precision. The character of the
agency bears no proportion to the magnitude of its
work. These low, unconscious forms of intelligence,
which inspire the plant cell to build up its fanciful
elevations, and the infinitesimal atom to seek after
and embrace its affinity, are precisely the same as
that which directs the sea of worlds upon their swift
and unvarying paths. And yet with all their exact-
itude and infinity of scope, they are as much below
that independent, self-conscious intelligence which
guides our thoughts and actions, as the protoplasm
is beneath the most highly organized and perfect
form.

Your theology has degraded you with the belief
that you are mendicants, enjoying the favors of
life as mere concessions from an all-powerful and
exacting master; and that your position in the cos-

mos bears a close relation to the insignificance of
your material bodies, and your feeble power in the
stupendous energies which surround you. Your
science will elevate you with the knowledge that
you are peers in the great universe, and that your
stature has no comparative measure for its proportions in the height and breadth of your material
world. It will teach you that by slow degrees, and
through millions of ages, you have become that
elimination of the spiritual out of the vast number
of divided intelligences which have built up and
governed your natural world; that you are the
harvest and fruition of the innumerable lower intelligences, which were sown broadcast in the beginning
to do their potent work.

In pursuing these matters, your scientists will arrive at a number of important truths, entirely in opposition to some of your present apparently established theories. In your speculations touching the
future state, there is a tendency which I cannot
designate by any other name in your language than
narrowness. You have come so recently to realize
the immense sizes and distances of the heavenly
bodies, that their comparison with your former con-
stricted views in that direction has produced a sense
of helplessness in the attempt to fathom these infinite spaces. But ages of contemplation will serve
to broaden your views, as well as to expand your

hopes. Encompassing or beside this broad universe we have evidence of a spiritual region, like the firm land bordering upon your own great ocean, which great body of water to the lower animal life within it is just as limitless and profound as the great cosmos is to yourselves.

CHAPTER VII.

THE confidential relations between our government and people have given it a parental character. It has consequently been the study of our legislation for ages past to assuage, as far as possible, those natural evils which creep in as the result of unrestricted social forces. Regarding the whole mass of our inhabitants as a family, the government could never feel that its duty was faithfully performed, while a number of its people were, relating to the ordinary enjoyments of life, in a state of suppression from any removable cause. You began your civilization, just as we began ours, by the crystallization of society into two classes. Those who at first, by thrift, acquisitiveness, or strong arms, became possessed of sufficient property to escape the necessity of daily toil for the sustenance of life ; and those who, by the absence of these qualities or from other causes, were obliged from day to day to exercise their muscular and nervous energies for the benefit of those who found it profitable to use and pay for them. This condition of society is a natural and just one, and there is nothing whatever in it to prevent the largest possible amount of happiness to all. But before many ages we discovered that the interests of the property class and the labor class were not equally equipped to maintain a fair and equitable relation with each other. We found that the interests of labor in the many bore no comparison in its political weight with the great power of wealth in the few ; and foreseeing that subjugation in time, of one by the other, which your experience has shown, we made wide provision against it.

We acknowledge as the foundation of all material progress that the honest accumulation of wealth should be the privilege of all ; and that the rights of property should be protected, and the enjoyment of it secured to everyone. Yet with these principles firmly and successfully carried out in our government, we have, for many centuries, considered it necessary to support and sustain the interests of the labor class by special legislative attention. You have pursued a directly opposite course. From the beginning of your history the privilege of wealth to hold labor in subjection, and to use it as an instrument of accumulation, with about the same regard for its well being as the horse in the collar or the ox under its yoke, has prevailed, without the enactment of any sincere and effective law to assist and sustain it in its unequal contest. On the contrary, your statute books are filled with oppressive laws against the labor class ; and while in your most civilized districts these unjust enactments are nearly

obsolete, there yet remains an average over your
planet of such legal and social suppressions of the
class whose strong arm supports you, as to be reck-
oned by us as the most unhappy and discreditable
feature of your social state.

It matters not how your economists may examine
and discuss the relations of labor with its co-operative interests, so long as they offer no proposals of
relief to it in the unjust burthen it bears of the hardships of life. Your common view that labor must
be unavoidably submitted to the law of supply and
demand, and that, consequently, eighty per cent of
your people are to be helplessly left to take their
chances of distress and suffering at each unfavorable
turn of the labor market, is peculiar to the planet
upon which you live, and is one of the most mistaken and unwise conclusions among you. This
heartless notion of yours is plainly the inheritance
of your early cruel ages. With such a state of things
you can never have a very high state of civilization.
With so many of you constantly under the vicissi-
tude of such adverse changes of condition, there
can be no steady progress of the whole, but little
encouragement to thrift ; a lack of ambition must
prevail in all the higher purposes of life, and a general surrender to improvidence and the vices which
follow. For that class which has created your
wealth, and is constantly renewing it, and which

constitutes so large a portion of your whole population, you can show nothing of legislative effort in
its favor except indirectly, through some of the purposes to smooth the way and increase the profits of
capital. The opportunities of your comparatively
small capitalistic class to use for its purposes, in an
entirely heartless way, the larger body of wealth
producers, have been made easy by natural conditions which would have been removed or corrected
long ago, under a more humane and unselfish ad-
ministration of your affairs, and if your governments
had not been exclusively in the hands of the smaller
class mentioned. We know of nothing more heartless and cruel of the governing classes of the earth,
than their careless submission of its wage-earners to
the unrestricted influence of competition for employment, under the compromising condition of a
necessity for bread.

In our philosophy we recognize only two honest
ways of accumulating wealth. One is the saving of
wages, and the other the profits of capital; and our
legislation has been chiefly directed to make the
chances of wealth by these two methods as even as
possible. To perform this service effectually, our
greatest efforts have been directed toward the labor
interest. We feel ourselves justified in this, because
the welfare of about seven-eighths of our people is
connected with this interest; because to the labor

class is entirely due the creation and constant re-
newal of all the wealth on our planet. Because, also,
that capital has natural advantages over labor, which
are first, its choice of time and place for investment ;
second, its capacity to wait for opportunities without the risk of physical suffering by its owners, and
the leisure for thought and knowledge it affords to
those who control it. Also, that capital, holding the
position of a voluntary employer, naturally assumes
the rights and privileges of master, which labor, in
its constrained and dependent situation, is obliged to
acknowledge.

We have long since considered these unequal relations and tendencies, and have proceeded to remedy them. Our legislation in behalf of the labor
classes is the happiest and most satisfactory of any
that we have. Without it our present civilization
would be impossible. Before describing our methods,
let me direct your attention to the immediate and
indirect causes which **bear** down upon the labor
classes of your planet.

Prominent among these is the promiscuous ownership of land. The surrendering of the Earth's
surface to the control of individual ownership is one
of the most serious mistakes of your civilization. It
is not to be mentioned alone as the greatest objection
to this, that the planet upon which you were born is
the natural inheritance of all of you, from whose

surface each and every one of you is destined to derive a sustenance, and that a monopoly of it by the few is as plain a violation of justice as it would be to hold the atmosphere in private use by sections, were such a thing possible. But it is chiefly to be taken into consideration, that your land policy enables the few to dominate the many, suppresses one class and elevates another, and insensibly transfers an undue portion of the earnings of labor into the pockets of your landholding classes.

Almost every influence now at work in the progress of your society tends to throw money into the hands of your land holders, not fairly earned by themselves. While the products of labor are cheapening from day to day, partly due to increased skill, and the appliance of machinery in their manufacture, and partly, also, by the competition of labor, owing to increase of population, yet even by these very operations the value of landed property goes up.

You already estimate rent as a considerable element of cost in the production of your food materials, and you are gradually approaching a period, when by the growth of population the cost of food will be very much increased by rent charges. You have all along submitted to this monopoly of land from causes plainly apparent. In the early days of your history all private ownership of land was acquired

and held by force, and it may be safely asserted that
no title at present exists in any of your older countries that is not founded on violent conquest, and
that has not been maintained by an organized and
armed authority, whose existence depends upon re-
taining the system of ownership in vogue. It is
plain to see that when the demand of justice to all
shall be the basis of political action, and especially
when the cost of your food supply shall become
greatly increased by the charges of rent, your present system will not be quietly endured.

In your own more favored region of the Earth
may be found temporary conditions which tend not
only to tolerate your present land ownership system,
but to render it popular. Your large area of unoccupied agricultural surface, from which any of your
citizens are permitted at small cost to select a portion with a title in perpetuity, destroys for the time
being the monopolizing character of private ownership; and while these governmental acts of land
distribution are the most remarkable concessions to
labor in human history, we fail to discover anything
in the practice but a temporary compromise between
the interests of capital and labor. As your society
progresses you must arrive at the time when your
landless class will be as effectually excluded from
the privilege of ownership as they are at present in
the older countries of the world.

Your own country in the newness of its human possession, by the lavish distribution of its territory into private hands, has alleviated the burdens of labor elsewhere, as well as within itself. It has effected this in two ways : first by withdrawing from the surplus population of densely inhabited districts abroad, and second by supplying from its rich agricultural lands a cheaper food supply to the older countries of the Earth than they were able to furnish from their own soils. But the most unreasonable among you cannot fail to perceive the speedy limit to these operations in the interests of labor, which after all must be considered as merely effecting a truce between that conflict of the laboring and landless many and the land-holding few which your people will surely witness in time. We manage these things very differently on Mars.

CHAPTER VIII.

THE planet Mars is held to be the inheritance of
those who are born upon it. Admitting the self-
evident and uncontrovertible justice of this view,
our government ages ago assumed the ownership
and property control of it in trust for the equal benefit of all. It has proceeded in accordance with this
view to grant its uses for all the purposes of industry
and pleasure, in such a manner as to bestow the income of its rent equally upon every living inhabitant.
I can only give you some outlines of our admirable
manner of accomplishing this purpose.

Our agricultural districts are divided into small
farms, even in size, with graded rents in accordance
with the richness of their soils, and other conditions.
Sub-letting is not allowed, and a chief purpose in
making these allotments is, that the family residing
upon each farm will be able to perform all the labor
required.   This is in accordance with a principle
which our government carries out in all possible
ways, to bring labor and capital into partnership.
The cultivator of the soil goes on with his improvements, in the assurance that they are as secure to him
as though his title were perpetual ; for in the event
of a change of tenancy, which is exceedingly rare,

a fair value is returned to him for all the fixed property which is the product of his labor. It is provided that there shall be no competition in the occupancy, and as the rent is but a nominal sum, he feels
no insecurity in his possession. Agricultural rents
are graded annually, and are payable shortly after
harvest. They may be either higher or lower than
those of the preceding year, depending entirely on
profits.

Landlordism, as it exists with you, is unknown
amongst us. The rapacity which under your unjust system is admitted to an ownership in which
no competition can possibly exist, and at the same
time is permitted to avail itself of that unlimited
competition which the pressure of public necessity
induces, has neither foothold nor abiding place
upon our planet. Under our system, you will
perceive that any increase of the profits of land is
met by the tenant with an increase of rent, and all
those natural causes which advance the value of landed property add to the government income, and in
that way are shared by all. Our government
derives its sole support from rent, and no other tax
or exaction is known. With a percentage of the
profits from the use of the land, which is never
burdensome to the tenant, it has been enabled, and
has found it to its interest, to carry out agricultural
and municipal improvements and enterprises which

individual ownership would never undertake. It
has drained our marshes, and reclaimed our desert
lands in the most efficient manner, without the
necessity of creating, as with you, an exacting
monopoly, which would claim of industry its lion's
share of profits from the work.

The government interest in our municipal progress, by virtue of its holdings, has led it to carry
out in the most complete manner those sanitary
enterprises which render city life safe and enjoyable. With its advantages of sole ownership of city
land, it is enabled to enforce certain uniform rules
of taste in house and street construction, which
have made our cities as complete and harmonious
as single works of art; their symmetrical combinations of lines and curves as consistently meeting
each other as in a separate architectural elevation.

As I have already hinted to you, a cultivation of
the beautiful in art and nature is a part of our
religion, and we indulge in the gratification of
esthetic inclinations as one of the greatest charms
of life. Our government erects no buildings except
public ones, and in their construction and fittings
is manifested that universal love of the grand and
beautiful which everywhere prevails. Your imagination is scarcely able to conceive the magnificence
of our temples of worship, and the charming perspectives of our streets and highways. Yet even

our industrious attention to all this pleasing effect
for the eye is held to be a matter of secondary importance, when compared with the health-giving
measures and regulations which prevail.

From the ground rents alone of every municipality, free and abundant water, light and heat are
supplied to every inhabitant ; and from the same
source of income a complete insurance is furnished
against individual loss from accidents, and all our
dead are disposed of without cost to relatives or
friends. We place no dead bodies in the earth as
you do, considering such a practice not only barbarous, but dangerous to the health of the living.
On the contrary, we extinguish them in a manner
which you cannot follow from a lack of the required
advance in chemical science. Ever since our discovery of the elementary unit we have had the
power to reduce all matter into its original state,
and it serves us well, that with our chemical
appliances and with due solemnity not a vestige of
the dead is left to be preserved, except their memories.

For the purpose of exhibiting to you the marked
difference of effect on labor and industry between
private and government ownership of land, let us
trace the institution and progress of one of your
cities in comparison with one of ours. These combinations of individual enterprise are to be found

upon your planet in all stages of growth, and may be most conveniently observed by you in this vicinity in their earlier periods of development. They are instituted mostly with you in a fortuitous way, a few individual interests forming the nucleus around which capital and labor are attracted, under the outlook of increased population and trade, to supply and create the various products of industry demanded. The whole land surface of your new city, including its prospective limits, is immediately appropriated at a trifling cost, by a single one or a small number of owners, under laws conveniently designed for their purposes. From this time forward the most extraordinary exactions from industry begin. Every stroke of the hammer and revolution of the fly wheel adds to the value of these possessions, until in a short time there is no limit to the price or rent of them, but the ability of industry to stand the tax.

During the earlier stage of your city's growth, conditions exist which disappear later. Labor is specially favored. The demand for it is as great as the supply, if not greater, and its savings enable it to get a share, by small investments, in the steady advance of land values. Your new city, supposing it to be a metropolis, is invested with all the elements of prosperity. Capital comes to it abundantly from abroad, induced by the opportunities of profitable investment, and labor is equally attracted by high pay. Population increases, together with all the enterprises of industry, and your land, conveniently divided into small lots, changes hands from one purchaser to another, each realizing a satisfactory and handsome profit. The monopolizing influences of land ownership are not generally felt, because of the large and unoccupied area of surface, and the facility to all in the acquirement of titles. Labor enjoys an era of remarkable prosperity outside as well as within the limits of your city. Your government has donated to it millions of acres of fertile agricultural lands, whose surface, for the most part, requires no great outlay of capital to fit it for the uses of husbandry ; and altogether, the general contentment and thrift indicate that all material interests are equally equipped and uniformly successful in the struggle of life. Labor goes cheerfully to its daily toil, and returns to its abundant board with a hope and ambition it has seldom known before. All human purposes appear in a flourishing state, except, it may incidentally be observed, that your religion at this period droops, without its usual attention and support.

You are now, we shall suppose, at the end of the second decade in the history of your city, and many changes are observable, due to the progress of your society and civilization. Your metropolis may con-

tain now about one hundred and fifty thousand
inhabitants. The market value of its land surface,
about three miles square, has increased, from the
government price at which it was purchased by the
single or half dozen purchasers, from about seven
thousand to three hundred and fifty millions of
dollars, and the whole value of the products of
industry upon it may be reasonably estimated at a
like sum. With the privileges and partnership
which labor has enjoyed in this great increase of
values, it is so far quiet and satisfied; but unfortunately the inevitable outcome is not so promising
to it. The evil effects of your private ownership
become more and more apparent as your city advances, and when, under the promptings of human
greed and selfishness, your landlords have fairly commenced their raid upon the industries of the city.
They now exact from you a tax in the form of land
rent alone which consumes yearly the twentieth part
of all the products of industry upon their possessions. This enormous tax is exacted without the
return of any service whatever except the privilege
of a dwelling place.

Your inhabitants are called upon also to provide
for the necessities of government, and an additional
tax is levied therefor, which takes from the profits
of labor and capital an amount equal to the tenth part
of all their savings. Because the privilege of becom-

ing a land owner is equal to all, and is the hope of most of you, you have permitted the transformation of this gift of nature-land into a monopoly, the most arbitrary and consuming that can be conceived.

This gift of nature, however, is not the only one diverted from its equitable distribution, and permitted to become the material of unrighteous exaction. The process of the water, heat, and light supply, so manifestly among the duties of your government to institute and superintend, is given, like your land, to the management and control of private individuals ; thus converting these indispensable elements of life and comfort into money getters for wealth, and subtracting to an unnecessary degree from the profits of industry and the savings of labor.

We shall now suppose that your city has arrived at the termination of its fourth decade. Its population has increased two-fold, and its land value has quadrupled ; but it is noticeable that your products of industry have not kept pace in their value with this enormous appreciation, and your ground rents alone now consume every ten years the whole cost of all buildings and their contents. In other words, every vestige of the accumulated labor of your city goes into the pockets of its landlords every ten years. Changes now become apparent in social life.

Competition has now reduced the wages of labor, and it has very nearly lost its ability to share in some of the minor operations of capital. The struggles of increasing numbers, precisely the same influence which has depressed wages, have advanced land. Labor has lost much of its old buoyancy and hopefulness. While raiment and food, the products of its own industry, have fallen in price, with a tendency to make up for its reduced income, every other one of its living expenses is greatly increased. Allowing it its proper place with matrimonial ambitions and hopes, the remarkable proportion of one fourth of its hard-earned wages is demanded of it in land rent alone, for a dwelling spot in the midst of a region which nothing else but its own energies have produced from a wilderness. Every single one of the bounties of nature, except the air and sunshine, are inacessible without the charges of an intercepting medium. The heat, and light-giving materials of the earth, together with water, the most useful and abundant of all, are served out to it burdened with all the costs and profits levied by an organized and irresponsible few.

The capital engaged in your industries adjusts itself to all these burdens, and is quiet under them, because it can readily reimburse itself by transferring all expenses and costs to prices. There is no such escape for labor, which not only pays these monopoly exactions directly, but as a consumer is obliged by an indirect method to foot a large share of these bills for capital. Capital remains contented under these extraordinary demands for another reason. All monopoly enterprises, and especially that one of land, furnish the safest and most profitable reservoirs of investment for its surplus earnings, and when it does not already participate it looks forward to a partnership in their profits.

You can readily understand, then, why the toilers of your city, at this period of its history, should show signs of sinking back into that dependent condition which characterizes them elsewhere upon your planet. A few among them, with great fortitude of restraint and large acquisitiveness, manage to lay by some of their earnings, but the margin between income and expense is so narrow that such a practice is not general. So that from the disabling vicissitudes of life, and a carelessness of habit induced by lack of ambition, comes that distressful state of existence, unknown on our planet, but common enough on yours, where a human being, with abundant stores of food and raiment surrounding him, suffers for enough of them to supply his moderate wants. Poverty, which before had been only exceptional and sporadic, assumes now the proportions of a numerous class among you, and out of which, by a lack of the opportunities of knowledge,

crime as naturally appears as weeds in a neglected
husbandry.

Another and significant change now becomes apparent in your social state. During the first stages
of your city's existence, there had been no money
invested except as capital. Every dollar laid out in
that way had been shared by labor. Any increase
in the volume of capital brings a corresponding
prosperity to those who toil; but the accumulations
from the profits of capital have not generally been
added to it, and in many cases the capital itself has
been led away into the many profitable monopoly
enterprises which abound. These now flourish as
they never did before. Increase of population and
trade has stimulated the various industries to increased supplies, but the prices of all commodities
instead of being raised are lowered. The free and
open competition within the precincts of capital and
labor has effected this ; not greatly to the detriment
of either, because the producer in one department
of industry is a consumer in many of the others, and
capital has increased its volume of business to make
up for smaller profits. But you have within the
borders of your city those money-making contrivances peculiar to your planet, wherein the natural
effect of competition is entirely reversed, and where
the universal law of supply and demand is com-

pletely abrogated. The worst and most disastrous of these is your system of land ownership.

Into this, and the other of your monopolies, capital pours its surplus, and finally retires to them with its accumulations, deserting its partnership with labor, and appearing on the scene in the new form of wealth. From a few instances, so rare as to be conspicuous, your holders of large money accumulations become now a numerous and influential class. While your society at one end has been sinking into poverty, it blossoms at the other with signs of unusual thrift. With an increase of luxury on one hand, and of want on the other, your city is now approaching the normal state. A few decades more it will have established within itself those relations between wealth, capital, and labor which are as inevitably the outcome of your land ownership system, as drouth and famine are the outcome of a lack of moisture in the soil.

We shall say now that your city contains a half million of inhabitants. Its surface is not extended in proportion with its increase in population, the cost of space inducing a greater crowding of houses and people. Your labor products, and the land upon which they rest, have been so constantly receding from each other in values, that now, with all the forced economy of space, your piles of goods, merchandise, and houses, if sold at their market value, would not furnish more than a quarter enough of money to purchase the ground beneath them. This enormous increase in the value of your city land is mostly the result of the opportunities its owners enjoy to prey upon the industries, and at this stage the following very remarkable conditions may be observed. While the city's capital, properly so called, is about three hundred millions of dollars, and the number of its workers in industrial pursuits about one hundred thousand, the aggregate earnings of both labor and capital combined have one quarter of the whole swept away by the demands of your landlords, estimating ground rent alone. And this enormous exaction, remember, is imposed without rendering any service in return. None of your economists will deny that this large drain does not come directly from the industries of your people, and its exhausting effects are daily seen in the gradually hardening lines in the lives of those who toil. In an early period, twenty persons in every hundred of your workers owned a portion of your city's surface. Now only four per cent are land owners, and within a few decades not more than five in a thousand will dwell or pursue their avocations without the virtual consent of some superintending ground owner, upon whose mercy in abstaining from ejectment or extortion they will remain in constant uncertainty.

The ownership of your city lots will now have gone almost exclusively into the hands of your leisure class; and the vast sums of money drawn monthly for rent, instead of being, as formerly, partly returned as capital, to assist labor in the various industrial enterprises is now either dissipated in luxury, expended in new possessions, or invested in some of the many monopoly undertakings of the day. The effects of this unjust burden are daily apparent. It reduces the possible savings of labor and the accumulations of industry to such a minimum that success in these is the exception rather than the rule. It is mostly because of this monopoly of land that life among your masses is a continuous and uninterrupted struggle; and to this more than all else is due that unequal distribution of wealth which affords only the few that cultivation and knowledge which elevates them, and that dooms the many to an unceasing wear of nerve and muscle to sustain themselves.

You cannot fail to have observed, as one of the most promising signs of your destiny, that wherever humanity in the midst of civilization is freest from the cares of sustenance supply, it inclines to devote its leisure to a cultivation of the mind. The crudeness and vulgarity of some, and the refinement of others, are entirely due to difference in opportunities of development, and between these two there must always exist a great repulsion. What good can you therefore expect of mankind as a whole, so long as by your methods a few only are vouchsafed the opportunities for knowledge?

The forces at work within your society have now, we will say, brought up your population and general conditions to the standard of those which may be found in the older portions of the Earth. Your poverty is more intense and widespread, with its corresponding increase in crime, while your wealth has become more munificent and ostentatious. Impelled by the necessities of life and a brave emulation, all your industries will be found in the highest strain of action. The accumulated products of labor and its multiplied activity have given to you a semblance of prosperity and success. But while in the course of your progress you have created new necessities and wants, you have made no just provision by which they could be, as near as possible, equally shared ; and as a consequence the apparent as well as the silent and concealed miseries of human life were never greater.

There is to be observed now a marked increase in the spread and influence of your religion. As the hope of success in life becomes lessened, and as the heartaches and distresses increase by your uneven struggles, the suffering and disappointed masses turn naturally to another existence for what has been denied them in this; and it can be said of all your religious theories, that their contrivances to make you suffer uncomplainingly the outrages of authority are the best that could have been devised. The few among you enjoying the bounties of life, surrounded by that want and privation whose voices they cannot escape, and whose strong arms they cannot fail to observe, turn instinctively to your religious doctrines with a sense of safety and protection. The few favored ones, looking over the vast multitude of their less fortunate brothers, are conscious that the superabundance they enjoy has been doubtfully acquired, and they are quick to embrace that convenient justification, which ascribes the greater ills and burdens of the many to a preconceived and unalterable arrangement of the divine will.

CHAPTER IX.

BEFORE bringing into comparison one of our cities it will be necessary to explain to you some of the processes which have rendered our present civilization possible. You already have a hint, from what I have said, of the very striking difference between the society of Mars and that of the Earth, in their handling of labor interests. While with your careless and indifferent treatment, labor remains degraded, we have raised it to a point of honor. We have arrived at our methods of its treatment by that philosophical induction which has interpreted to us the many reliable and unerring decrees of the divine will. Nature, upon whom we depend for all we know of the supreme wishes, has furnished indubitable signs that diligence is a saving and wholesome quality, inseparable from intelligence, in its extended sense as we know it, upon which the very existence of all material things rests. But even the activities of nature are not more indispensable to the firmness of the Earth, than individual mental and physical energy is to the well-being and progress of your society. Since one of these energies is as useful as the other in the economy of the world, we can conceive no reason why you should allow

one of them to dominate the other ; nor how you
can justify yourselves in bestowing upon one all the
honors and emoluments, while to the other you
pursue a course denying opportunities, and in all
ways bringing upon it an inferior social scale.

We met these natural tendencies ages ago, by a
determination to equalize, as far as possible, the
burdens of life among all classes, and to this end we
have chiefly directed our efforts to sustain the interests of those who, by a struggle for the necessities of life, are obliged to toil.   Some very remarkable results have followed.   We have achieved that
degree of justice where the skillful artisan, by
virtue of his manual cunning alone, can acquire a
certain elevation in our society, and whose occupation is not subordinated by any other on our planet.
We have a very numerous class amongst us, known
by the best interpretation of your language as cap-
tains of industry, who secure truer and more lasting
honor than your military heroes.   Our admiration
of them arises from the fact that they assist to build
up and restore the waste of those industrial products
which sustain our lives.   By methods, long ago in
vogue, we have united our intellectual and manual
training so that there should be no social separation
between them. But while equal distinction awaits
the skillful pursuit of either path, the highest honors
are achieved by those who excel in both.   Conse-

quently our youth, encouraged by their parents and teachers, become emulous of the qualities of physical endurance attached to labor, and serve their terms among the toilers with a will that nothing but a high ambition could create. This greater respect and consideration for physical industry than yours would have been impossible, were it not that we have avoided the various causes which either suppress or degrade it. In the first place, we have decreed that it shall receive a fair share of its earnings. Chiefly in furtherance of this, we have ordained that no individual holder of land shall rob it by taking to himself that appreciation in values which its diligence produces. To this end also we have provided that wealth and capital shall not bear down upon it in the various monopoly exactions common with you. But a measure of justice, scarcely less effectual than these to elevate and sustain labor, is our governmental system of fixing its rates of wages.

From what has been said it will not be hard for you to believe that a working man holds a very different position in society with us than with you. Upon the Earth, driven by the necessities of life, and a cruel and unrestrained competition, he is obliged to forego nearly all those opportunities which refine and elevate the mind. He has little of leisure, without the depression of muscular fatigue.

His habiliments are the badges of inferiority in your social scale, and he trudges along on his tiresome, hopeless journey, bearing his condition as one under the prohibition of better things by an inexorable fate. No competency rewards his unremitting toil, though with the skill of his hands he is building the wealth of the world. To the sordid and cunning comes fortune in possessions and estates; while to him comes only the privilege to dwell in another's house, and to partake of that fare whose chief quality shall be its capacity to restore the wasting energies of his body.

With us the pursuit of manual labor is attended with better conditions. By securing to industry its rightful rewards, it has been adopted by choice instead of compulsion, as the best way to gain independence. Having no road to wealth, except through the sterling qualities of industry and prudence, industry and probity are the indispensable qualities which lead to the upper stratum of our society. Thus, you will perceive, the natural laws of progression and development are encouraged to work out their beneficent results in the life of every individual.

Since, from the cradle to the grave, all are surrounded with the living rewards of goodness, we have no need of sermons. We know no gilded vice. It bears no fruits with us but destruction. You preach against it and reward it in the same breath. You denounce it in empty words, and at the next moment honor it with a bow. You sanc-tion the wholesale injury which your system inflicts upon each one, hoping in the scramble to pocket the losses of others. The most desirable condition of life with you is that in which the attainment of wealth shall furnish personal gratification, the ac-complishment of which, in most cases, is through a line of public and private wrongs. The better con-ditions of life with us are acquired in the fertiliza-tion of innumerable schemes for the common wel-fare.

You are not to make the mistake of supposing that our society has arrived at the dead level of equality. We have no castes, as you have, holding apart from each other with marked distinctions of wealth. But we have social grades, as you have, with the great difference that each one enjoys un-envied the pleasures within reach ; not the least of which is to share the cares as well as the delights of life with each other. The feeling of contempt for one another is entirely unknown among the peo-ple of Mars. We have provided that there shall be no unlettered and vulgar substratum in our society to pity or condemn, as you have. The even justice of our system has bestowed upon all equal oppor-tunities of knowledge and cultivation. As a result, there is no individual living upon our planet who is superior to another, except by a more assiduous exercise of mental or physical gifts, or a higher cultivation of his spiritual nature.

A marked indication of our advanced social development is, that we utterly refuse the performance of any act which is an injury, even in a remote degree, to our fellows ; while in the intense selfishness of your present state, you are constantly sacrificing each other's interests. With sentiments like these prevailing, it is easy for you to understand why we have no class among us perpetually under less favored conditions than another class, and why, acting under the great lesson of nature which has sent us all into life upon an equality, we have ordained in all possible ways that the journey thereafter shall be fair and equal to all.

It is not possible for you to thoroughly understand or appreciate what I am about to lay before you, in a description of our society in municipal life, without a further knowledge of some of our methods. One of the most important of these, is the perfection which we have brought to our science of statistics, and the indispensable service it is made to perform in our political economy. This branch of science is pursued by us as the most serviceable and practical of all. We learn from it in a positive way many truths which your economists fail to reach, and we have discovered by it many errors which have existed as the result of sophistical reasoning. We use it as a rule and square to measure the speculations of philosophy, as well as an every-day guide in the practical affairs of life. Its better value for us lies in the fact that our conclusions from it are adduced out of the records of centuries. It is to social science what analysis is to chemistry. It is only by a systematic and orderly record of the occurrences of nature, and the changes and events of society, that we have arrived at the many profound truths so deeply concerning our lives. By it we have discovered how astonishingly nature holds, concealed from common eyes, so many of her processes, coquetting with us, as it were, in witholding her greatest favors without prolonged and incessant interrogation. But although our store of scientific knowledge has been increased by these statistical labors, we hold them of no less importance in managing the practical affairs of life.

Our bureau of statistics is without question the most valuable department of our government. It has been brought to its perfected condition by centuries of practice and improvement, and upon it rests, in a great measure, the prosperity and happiness of our people. By it, mainly, we are enabled to save our population from the distresses of overproduction, and the chance occurrences of uneven labor demand. Your experience has shown you that in times of depression the causes were plainly apparent. We have merely arranged to anticipate these causes, to sound the general alarm, and to forestall them. Outside of the defects of your currency, and your speculation, which are your most prolific sources of industrial disaster, comes that blind over-production, entirely undirected by any reliable or authoritative knowledge of the existing capacity to consume. You are having at times a large amount of misdirected labor in the form of products slow of sale; and for the time being a supply, so much in excess of demand, does not return a full equivalent for the labor invested. These frequent errors of production depress wages, and are altogether more calamitous to labor than to capital; because labor is variously skilled, and cannot readily transplant itself from one department of production to another, and is obliged, under the conditions, either to accept reduced wages or to remain idle. Capital does not suffer as labor does in these constantly occurring over-supplies. On the other hand, it finds its opportunity, either by waiting from a low to a high market for its returns, or by changing its field of investment. In these frequent partial or complete suspensions in the production of over-supplied commodities, labor is therefore the chief sufferer.

We have nearly a complete remedy for this in our

system of statistics. Our planet in all its habitable parts is divided into districts, in each of which is kept an accurate and systematic record of all available labor, as well as an account of its different classes, with the separate capacity of each for production. In connection therewith is also kept an account of all products turned out. The information furnished in this way determines the surplus or deficiency of all commodities produced. We are enabled thereby to know, almost at a glance, the drift of all labor energies, and to direct them safely from any great redundancy of supply. When engaged in the production of food supplies, where nature becomes of necessity a party to this great co-operative arrangement, we have devised a method that saves those who toil from the embarrassment and the frequent distress of an intermittent cost of living. We had observed that the tendency of cheap food to lower the wages of labor, and of dear food to raise them, was not equal, wages being much more easily lowered than raised under this natural influence. Our government has undertaken therefore to establish a fair and equitable adjustment between the cost of living and wage rates, to be modified when occasion requires.

You are not to expect me to go into detail in these matters; but as it may seem impracticable to you, how any arbitrary rate of wages may be made to rule fairly among so many different people, I will

give you some account of our system of grading
labor, by which this difficulty is overcome. We have
formed out of the three qualities of *skill, strength*
and *activity* a basis upon which to reckon the value
of all individual labor. Each of these is divided into
three grades, and the highest valued workman is he
who stands first in all. The first grade of skill is
considered equal to both the first and second grades
of strength and activity in estimating wages; and
there is no first grade of skill allowed, except in
those industrial operations requiring much manual
training. The workman begins his career usually in
the lowest grades of each, although at times strength
and activity are raised one grade at the beginning.
The wages of all labor are uniformly established by
the government, in accordance with the standing of
the individual and the certificate he holds, according
him his status under this method of estimating his
ability. From middle life to old age changes usually
occur in his grade, and his apportionment of wages
is consequently modified; but so long as he retains
his skill it goes far to keep up the allotment of fair
wages against the loss of strength and activity.

This is merely an outline of our system. Its importance will be understood, when you consider
that by it we have established a uniform rate of
wages for all, and have saved our workmen from
helplessly submitting themselves to the natural

competition of dependent numbers, and to the exacting patronage of a selfish and independent few. Although we have achieved this desideratum of uniform wages, we are not unaware of the economic impossibility of rendering them constant, and we have accordingly arranged that the rate shall be changed to correspond with the varying cost of living. Each year, therefore, after the gathering of our harvests, our statistical bureau makes its report of food supply ; when any change, if necessary, is made in the rate of wages for the ensuing year, thereby determining that labor shall enjoy a fair share of the wealth which it produces.

Outside of the handicraft of the workmen, we have established a scale for estimating a just rate of pay for all employees in professional and business pursuits. This arrangement is based upon the qualities of *talent, intelligence* and *capability*. Each one of these is divided into three grades, and whoever stands first in all of them is entitled, of course, to the highest pay for his services. Usually, however, these high qualifications secure a reward beyond the scale. This system of rewarding labor has a far-reaching effect in our political economy, and is in complete uniformity with the general tendency of our efforts to promote steady values. The most important element of cost in all commodities offered for sale is labor, and that can never be cheapened. We have not a single product of industry in our list which represents in its labor cost, as many of yours do, the underpaid, gaunt and hopeless toil of some fellow creature struggling for the scanty means to live.

Owing to our many concessions physical industry has been curtailed of that excessively wearisome and exhausting character known to you. Without the oppressions which bear down upon it on your planet, its pursuit never reaches that forced extremity which brings the bent form and care-worn face.

A considerate custom has fixed our period of daily labor at six hours ; one-half of which, under the equitable adjustment of our wage rates, affords sufficient pay, under ordinary circumstances, to furnish a liberal enjoyment of life. Under our system three hours of work each day affords a share of wealth somewhat in excess of the share usually obtained by the workmen of the Earth for their average of ten hours' labor. Our industrial force has, therefore, a facility of expansion and contraction, without distressful results, which yours does not possess. No serious changes are wrought with us by a reduction of working force to half time, and consequent half pay ; while more or less pinching and misery are sure to follow such an occurrence with you.

From these careful attentions to the interests of labor, we have brought it into repute as one of the most honorable as well as the most profitable pursuits of life. I have endeavored to show you some of the ways by which this grand purpose has been attained. I must not, however, omit to remind you, that as our government takes upon itself to perform innumerabie enterprises, which on the Earth are left to individuals and organizations of men, its direct dealings with those who toil are more intimate and extensive than yours. It is better enabled thereby to carry into operation those methods which distinguish our system. The greater part of the energies of our government and the wisdom of our statemanship has been directed to this end of supporting labor, and out of it, without question, comes the general serenity and contentment which prevail.

CHAPTER X.

WHEN it is decided by our authorities that a new
city shall be built to meet the requirements of increasing numbers, and to establish that convenient
co-operation in branches of industry and trade which
close association affords, its location is left entirely
to the judgment of a board of government officers, of
sanitary and civil engineering skill. If, as is frequently the case, the proposed site is already occupied by one or more tenants in rural pursuits, they
are scrupulously indemnified in all losses which result from their dispossession.

I wish to impress upon you here, that a tenant, under our government, has even greater security of
possession than your land owners. The prevailing
sense of justice, and a widespread interest, have
established the right of a renter to hold and enjoy,
against all competition, his allotment during his life.
He has also the right, under our custom, to convey
its possession by will ; and it is more generally the
case on our planet than on yours, that a piece of land
is held for generations in the same family. Our government exercises some rights of interference, to the
end that the size of a farm shall conform, as near as
possible, to such dimensions as to employ no great

excess of labor over that capable of being supplied by the family of the occupant. In a general way, the tenant enjoys the same rights of ownership which are held by your individual holders in fee, except that he cannot convey title, and does not take to himself any emolument arising from increased value. His rent is simply an equivalent to your tax, with the very important difference, that its amount depends entirely on the season's productiveness, and is never a burden.

Once decided upon, the proposed city becomes the subject of universal interest. Its plans are submitted and approved, just as your proposals for a single edifice. All its parts must conform with each other; the choice of its location chiefly depending upon drainage and water supply, it possesses these advantages in the highest perfection. Every house must be erected in conformity with rules. Work is commenced by the erection of public buildings in the center, and the laying of drain, water, heat and electric conduits through its newly surveyed streets. People come to it, as they come to your new cities, for the purpose of gain in trade and industry, and locate themselves as they choose under a fixed and uniform land rental. They erect edifices as you do, varying them as they like in their internal structure, but strictly conforming in their outer elevations to the style adopted by our architectural commission,

which supervises also the material employed, and
the safety and durability of the work. Any disrepu-
table or depraved quarter is of course impossible under this plan ; nor could such an encouragement and
propagation of crime exist in one of our cities, as they
do in yours, even had we the class of tenants to people them. It must be charged among the evils of
your landlordism, that it not only promotes vice
through its tendency to impoverish your masses, but
is ready at all times to multiply it, by affording quarters for convenient association.

The spectacle of our city in course of construction
is very different from yours. The government has
set aside, what may be computed in your way as
millions of money for the institution of various works
designed for the health and comfort of the new population, and people are arriving in thousands from
all quarters to do the work. Every one of them is
impressed with that feeling and interest which can
only arise from ownership, and there is not a single
one of them who is not performing some of the work.
No one of them has a hope for honor and wealth by
getting a monopoly of the land. No rich man comes
with his accumulations to get a perpetual lien upon
the industries that are just now springing up, and
to hold for himself and his descendants the privilege
of exacting daily for all time a larger share of the
earnings of labor than your slaveholders derive

from their human chattels. All choose to work, because it is both honorable and profitable to do so,
and also because it is a duty, the conscious fulfillment
of which is attended with a feeling of happiness.

The systematic and regular use of the voluntary
muscles, without excessive fatigue, has not only an
important influence on health, but assists as well to
develop perfect and well rounded brains, out of which
can only come those evenly balanced minds which
create, out of the power of intelligence, the blessings of human progress ; whence only come those
level headed men, who are distinguished among
yourselves as being never wholly the product of
learning. It is an axiom with us, that he who does
not produce has no right to consume, and this doctrine has been so carried out in our society that
physical inertia, no matter how much attended with
wealth, is exceedingly rare. As a consequence,
affluence with us is not beset with the terrible penalties of ill health. The muscular body in all conditions of life is made to act with the brain and nerves.

We shall suppose, now, our city has reached a
period of its growth equal in time to your decade.
Its grand temple is not quite completed. Its streets
stretch away in the distance, none of them narrower
than a hundred of your feet, and some of them
more than twice as wide, to accommodate the airships
and the larger warehouses. The lines of uniform

house fronts, relieved on the street corners by elevated towers, reach out sufficiently far into the gradually changing suburbs to give a hint of the long and beautiful perspectives that are to come. From the center outwards there are reserved, at intervals of about a half mile, spaces corresponding with the area of two blocks, which make a circular belt around the whole. These are cultivated and embellished in the highest style of gardening and landscape art. Here are located our public baths, statues, monuments, conservatories, and arenas for athletic sports. These pleasure grounds, so convenient and accessible, diversify our city life with a taste and flavor of the country. Our city grows in a solid expansion. There are no straggling suburbs, like yours. Blocks are erected together, and always in continuation of the appropriated space adjoining them. The intercourse and demeanor of our population are, as you may except, unlike yours. The general air of serenity and contentment, the uniform politeness, and the absence of degradation, with its frequent unpleasant and disgraceful episodes, mark the difference between your city population and ours.

It concerns us most, however, to make a comparison of our wealth producing agencies, and the channels of their distribution, and for this purpose we shall take our metropolis as it stands in its maturity. It contains, now, like your city of advanced growth, about three hundred thousand inhabitants. Its land rentals have been subjected to constant modification, and are in some places very much higher than they were at first. In certain localities, where trade has concentrated, the public fund has been increased by a considerable advance of rent to store keepers, but there is no exorbitant demand of rent for such favored places as there is with you. The purpose of rent with us being only to meet the expenses of government, its total is limited ; and consequently, while in the mercantile and trade districts, where wealth and capital are most heavily engaged, it has been materially advanced, a corresponding reduction has taken place in the residence portions. The direct and immediate effect, therefore, of an appreciation of land value, is to reduce living expenses among the masses by curtailing their rents. In the absence of any monopoly of private ownership, there is no case, even in the most concentrated places, where rent forms anywhere near so large a proportion of business expense as with you. By your land ownership methods, landlords have an access to both pockets of the tenant. Out of one they take to the limit of their greed whatever sum they choose for the privilege of business quarters, or a dwelling place, and from the other a tithe on everything consumed by the enhanced cost of its distribution.

As our material wants and needs are very much like yours, it is not hard to make a comparative estimate of the savings of industry. We produce more wealth than you in a given time, even with our shorter daily periods of work, because, with few exceptions, all are engaged in the business of production. By this increased productiveness every consumer is richer. He is able by a smaller amount of labor to procure a greater amount of the objects of desire. Our production is more perfect than yours, by the use of more perfect machinery. Our division of labor is more complete than yours. Our workmen having abundant leisure for intellectual development, all the practical advantages of knowledge and science are immediately brought into effect. By avoiding your great waste of capital by excessive government expenditures, it is constantly so abundant with us that its proportion to labor makes labor remunerative.

We have now assumed for the purpose of comparison that the two cities, one of Mars and one of the Earth, have each three hundred thousand inhabitants; and that, allowing for women and children not engaged in productive industry, one hundred thousand of each city is actively engaged in industrial pursuits. As the general prosperity of each

city depends upon the earnings of this one hundred
thousand, and the accumulations in capital and
wealth upon the amount saved by these productive
classes, let us make a relative estimate of the opportunities each possess in individual savings. Having
no common medium of exchange upon which to base
our estimate, let us take the value of a day's labor
for that purpose. The income of a city is derived
from two sources, the aggregate wages of its inhabitants, and the combined profits of its capital. The
latter, however, being entirely derived from consumers, is largely contributed to by the inhabitants
themselves. And for the reason that all imported
products, as well as those exported, bear the profits
of capital in their rates of sale, we may safely say
that an amount very nearly equal to the whole profits of capital of a city is paid by the consumers
within its limits as capital profits. The chief source
of your city's yearly income then is about thirty-one
million days' labor. Out of this you must pay for
expenses, under your system, two million days'
labor for government taxes, fifteen million days'
labor for ground rent, two million days' labor for
water, two million days' labor for insurance, and
with the balance of ten million days' labor you must
pay the cost of food, raiment, fuel, the portion of rent
estimated in buildings, together with the various
incidentals of furniture and house lights. You will

observe that all these expenses except the first are largely loaded with the profits of capital, so that with the income and expense as set forth you may be in a progressive condition, as that term is defined by you. That is to say, your capital may increase, and your wealth may be very greatly augmented. The enormous proportion of your earnings carried away by rent, although drawn very largely from your business districts, is contributed equally by the whole in the increased cost of all products consumed. Of your one hundred thousand producers, it is safe to say that twenty thousand of them have capital investments. Among these is divided the whole of the surplus of the city's earnings. The eighty thousand engaged in the business of directly creating wealth are doomed, under your cruel system, to sweat and toil from sun to sun without accumulations. You accept this condition of things as inevitable, and your economists contend that the real or natural remuneration of labor is the bare means of subsistence. We have seen the unrighteous origin of this prodigious fund, which absorbs one third of the earnings of labor at least: let us examine its perpetual effects upon the interests of those who toil.

Looking upon your civilization, we find in its modern aspects a wonderful increase in all the appliances and conditions which accumulate wealth.

Among these may be specified a better and more economical division of labor, the discoveries of science, labor saving inventions, and altogether as a result, greatly increased productiveness.

Added to these contributions of knowledge and science in the interest of the working class, you have, during the last century, experienced the most remarkable acquisition in favor of labor that was ever known upon your planet. I allude to the accession of new and fertile lands, over which the boundaries of civilization have been extended, and out of which, by the new methods and contrivances both of husbandry and transportation, the food supplies of the Earth have been made to flow in a steady stream toward the districts of their consumption. These immense advantages could not fail to have, in some degree, a beneficent effect upon your labor class. Inasmuch as your workmen of to-day are enabled to obtain more of the comforts of life than formerly, real wages may be said to have considerably advanced. Their share, however, of the wealth produced is as small a portion as formerly. By the modern necessities which custom has rendered difficult to avoid, they have become larger consumers, which in itself has enabled your capital, with its undue advantages, to increase its store out of all proportion to a fair division of the wealth produced. But the greater and cheaper food supply, and the

abundant capital of your recent times, while serving
to neutralize the depressing effect of increase of
population in the labor ranks, and to institute a
condition of general prosperity in trade and mercantile pursuits, has at the same time offered to all
your monopolists of land the opportunity to extort,
under the pressure of competition, the whole surplus of the earnings of your workmen. Precisely
the same happy conditions which have brought a
modicum of prosperity to them have created a richer
field for your monopolists, and especially for those
of them who by their ownership of city land can
exact from the extended demands of business, and
a rapidly multiplying population, an unfair portion
of the wealth produced. The unlimited privilege
of appropriating to themselves the utmost share of
the profits of industry, gives a speculative value
to the holdings of your landlords, and serves in
turn to furnish them the excuse of a parallel in
their charges for rent to the current rate of interest
on money. If industry can be forced to make over
to them a third of its earnings now, the possibilities
of the future shadow golden dreams, which promise
no less to them than the power of your imaginary
Midas—dreams which encourage an easier wealth-
making than was possessed by your olden barons,
who by force of arms were enabled to hold,—what

your modern law and custom equally allows,—the
privilege of sapping the industry of millions of busy
hands of all else but a bare sustenance and a shelter
from the elements.

That rent does not yet to any great extent enter
into the cost of your agricultural products, is due to
the abundance of new land coming constantly under
cultivation, and to that equalizing of situations
which your railroads promote.   An increase in the
demand for food, and the promise of an advance in
its price, brings under cultivation lands of lesser
fertility or those more remote from your markets.
The monopoly power of agricultural land ownership is thereby effectually destroyed.   So long as
these favorable conditions exist, the cost of your
food staples will be governed by the value alone of
the labor employed.   The profits of capital, therefore, take no part in them until they leave the
hands of the producer.   There is no value in your
cultivated lands of the lesser fertility, except in the
opportunity they afford for labor to exchange its
services for money.   This class of land fixes the
price of and cheapens the food of the Earth.   The
value of all lands from these upwards in degrees of
fertility is estimated by the amount of produce derived from a given amount of labor, and except in
a few favorite situations there is as yet no monop-

oly value in your cultivated lands. To this, more than anything else, is due the comparative cheapness of your food, and the steady and unrestricted increase of your population. In time, however, for reasons too obvious to require mention, rent must enter into the original element of cost among your food staples, just as it now so largely takes a part in the cost of their distribution. The fullest manifestation of the evils of your private ownership system will then take place. The signs of what may occur at that rapidly approaching critical period are to be seen in the completely merciless character of your wealth holders, who, in the face of a divine intelligence, which has so charitably provided an even abundance to all, attempt to subvert the natural laws of trade by unfair combinations, known among you as trusts and syndicates, wherein the common welfare is made a sacrifice to their determined and unscrupulous love of gain.

You have perhaps not fully considered how it has come to pass that your wealth is so generally without the best feelings and impulses of humanity. The desire to accumulate which pervades all classes can accomplish nothing in the ranks of labor, except for those who possess it in an inordinate degree. The anxiety for gain must be so intense as to overwhelm the wish for gratifications within reach, and to produce a fortitude of restraint which denies every dis-

pensable want and pleasure. It is only the few
who have this power of abstinence that can escape
a life of drudgery. The ranks of capital and wealth
are largely recruited from this body of abstainers.
Under the depressing effects of your monopolistic
condition, ordinary prudence and moderate abstemi-
ousness are not, as a rule, capable of laying the
foundation of wealth. You have, consequently, by
a natural process of selection, the ranks of your
moneyed classes filled up, for the most part, by the
most aggressively mercenary and acquisitive of your
race ; while the better part of humanity, where the
self-sacrificing and generous impulses most prevail,
must pay the penalty of their virtues in unrelieved
dependence. Your successful moneyed class, coming in time to that place of power which their
wealth procures for them, shape and direct your
legislation ; which, as you might expect, instead of
being devoted, as it should be, chiefly to the support of measures to equalize and ameliorate the conditions of all classes, works the machinery of government for their own selfish ends, making easy
and comfortable paths for those schemes which multiply their wealth.

While the wish to accumulate is acknowledged
to be the fountain head of all material progress,
its accomplishment, under your system, is mostly
the reward of those qualities of the mind which

are not safe lessons for common acceptance. Your examples of material success are not good studies, if charity and the true public spirit are to be considered as worthy of being enlarged by precept.

CHAPTER XI.

OUR more advanced civilization and truer democ-
racy exhibit themselves nowhere more strikingly,
than in the way in which we have determined the
equal division of land interests. With our city of
three hundred thousand inhabitants, and its income
during the same period of time as yours of thirty-
one million days' labor, there is assessed by our authorities about the sum as ground rent equivalent to
eight million average days' pay of our workmen.
For this amount in hand, our government furnishes
to its tenants, without further cost, perfected streets
in constant repair, abundance of water for household
and other purposes, lights both in houses and streets,
heat by our system (to you undiscovered), perfect
drainage without cost or repair of conduits, insurance against individual loss by fire or flood, free
burial to the dead, and a system of education bestowing upon every individual the higher branches
of study.

Besides this immense service, the government
provides religious edifices, buildings for public entertainment, and pleasure grounds. And all this,
you will bear in mind, at a less cost to our population than your landlords exact of you for ground rent

alone. Adding to this four million days' labor for rent, paid to private owners of buildings, and we have left nineteen million days' labor for living expenses not provided by our government, and out of which come all the profit and accumulations of capital, except those derived from rents of buildings. You will see thereby, that with all the monopoly privileges that have fastened themselves upon your system done away with, capital has yet a full scope to exercise its legitimate functions in the fields of production and distribution, apart from which it has no rights and is entitled to no legislative consideration.

It is only by expunging the demands and profits of capital that the government is enabled to furnish all these services mentioned at so small a cost. We hold it to be a principle of justice, that the natural elements should not be permitted to form the basis of corporate management or monopoly control, and therefore instead of allowing capital the fullest privilege to appropriate those bounties of nature which are found ready for use, we have restricted its operations to a mere partnership with labor, where it justly belongs. In our endeavors to sustain labor, and to equalize its opportunities with capital, we have gone much further than this. We hold that all public necessities of general demand, in the supplying of which large expenditures are required in fixed capital, and which are not strictly in the line of production, should be provided for by the government. We remove the burdens of labor, by relieving it of those large capital enterprises which subsist on it, and which fail to share with it a reasonable portion of earnings. The large sums of money and the special privileges required in these operations of supply, of which your railroads and telegraph lines are prominent examples, obstruct the natural tendency of competition, and capital and wealth are thereby permitted advantages over labor which they should not of right have.

The unlimited privilege of capital in these directions has been defended on the ground that it greatly accelerates your material progress; that in private hands these enterprises can be more economically managed; and that the centralization of power in a government would be dangerously increased by the proprietorship of such large undertakings. All of these allegations except the first are without foundation in fact. The growing political weight, especially in your representative governments, of all monopoly combinations, by reason of their wealth and large individual patronage, presents to you the choice of either a government ruled by outside influences, which cannot be held responsible for the evils it inadvertently inflicts by the irresistible pressure from without, or a government entirely and absolutely liable, and to be held to a strict accountability for all encroachments upon the common welfare while handling these services of supply. In the latter case your remedy is an easy one ; and may be readily applied ; while in the former, nothing short of a political convulsion will serve you. No advanced government upon your Earth has ever undertaken a public service of any magnitude for a long term, which has not been systematized and improved by all the available knowledge and science of its time. The difference between a public and a private supply of a common demand is, that to one is added the costs and profits of capital ; while the other, shorn of these oftentimes excessive exactions, is furnished at the cheapest rate possible.

Any policy of your governments, no matter how unwisely adopted, becomes in time a fixture which is difficult to remove. The abuses which it may be known to produce are tolerated long after its evil is understood. Yet, there is scarcely one of these which has not had its active defenders. The able defense of measures which have long since been expunged for their flagrant injustice, exhibit some of the most striking examples of mental obliquity in your annals. No government of the Earth, however, in its long legislative career, was ever known to favor the laboring and landless over the interests of those holding endowments of the Earth's surface.

What seems at a superficial glance to be in your own country such a measure, in what may be generally termed your land policy, with its homestead provisions, becomes upon a closer examination delusive. Every one of your laws for the pretended purpose of bestowing your territory upon labor bears the covert design of a connivance to further the opportunities of capital. From the inauguration of your system, capital and wealth have been gradually absorbing your lands, and the partnership of labor in them is as transitory and accidental as the opportunities afforded in the early stages of your city's growth.

The fact appears that, in your present development, the general sense of individual acquisitiveness among your governing classes is too great to deal fairly with the whole body of your people under such seductive opportunities for self-gain. You cannot prevent, under your present system of private ownership, the lands now held by your people from drifting into a comparatively few hands. This process, although going on for years, gradually accelerates, and will rapidly become apparent when the last of your public territory shall have passed out of the hands of your government. The owners of your lands always have, and will continue to govern the countries of the Earth. No representative government can exist long without a system which prevents the monopoly of its territory by wealth.

No other idea appears to have been held by the founders of your nation, but that your land was a chattel, to be disposed of for money, and as much a subject of barter and speculation as merchandise, and like it, liable to that depression in value which a superabundant supply produces. Its unequalled advantages as a subject for speculation became more and more apparent as your population increased. It is a striking illustration of the irrestible influence of the mercenary impulse on your planet, that those who were prominent in establishing so many advances toward equalizing the conditions and privileges of their fellowmen held, in the aggregate among themselves, the title and possession of which they stood ready to defend, an area of the Earth's surface equal to about eight million of your acres, one hundred thousand acres being in possession of him who became the first presiding officer of your republic. I do not refer to these facts in a spirit of censure to those men, so enlightened and liberty loving beyond their times ; but only to show that singular limit of vision which sincerely proclaimed the equality of all men, while fostering a political method which must in time enslave or pauperize the majority.

There can be no doubt but that the unlimited privileges of capital in these directions have greatly accelerated your material progress. The speedy utilization of the immense resources of your own republic has hidden and disguised the evil it was gradually producing. The new fields of labor opened by the many monopoly enterprises have satisfied and quieted it; and the open invitation, for the time being, of a partnership with capital in the occupancy of the soil for purposes of cultivation, leaves no apparent ground of complaint among the masses who toil. Thus have your demands for labor been so much greater than the supply, that large accessions have been drawn from the older countries of the Earth. These furnishing the bone and sinew for still more rapid development, your progress has become the wonder of the age. You will perceive, however, that the general prosperity among all classes of your society, and the absence of any great public grievance, is just that condition which render the incursions of capital and wealth easy, so that during all your enormous accumulations by the hands of your workers, out of which they have little to show of gain besides their living expenses, the most stupendous moneyed fortunes of history have fallen into the hands of the few. Unlike the older countries of the Earth, where the increasing poverty of the masses is a natural and unavoidable sequence of the large accumulations of wealth in few hands, your poor do not grow sensibly poorer during this unequal distribution. Your enormous resources hold up labor to a condition of comparative prosperity during all these inroads upon it. As a consequence, of the abundance which the bounties of nature have supplied to you, and the stimulated energies which your well rewarded industries have induced, your labor unconsciously submits to the extraction of an unfair portion of the wealth it produces without individual suffering. The better condition of your workmen compared with those of other lands should not disguise the fact, however, that capital and wealth get new assurance, and are encouraged to fresh demands upon the industries on this account. Although your poor do not yet grow sensibly poorer, your rich are getting immeasurably richer. The better opportunities for labor have brought millions of workers from abroad, who in their rapid development of the country have so immensely appreciated land values that the bosom of the Earth has been converted into a chattel for speculation, and the chief business of wealth has been to pocket the increase which it has not earned.

You cannot fail to have observed, that to this period your money class has had but little to do with land in your agricultural districts, except to buy and sell it. Capital, other than that limited quantity which has been created on the land, has not thus far been led into the business of its cultivation, because from the abundance and easy acquirement of land it must come, in so doing, in such direct competition with labor as not to leave a satisfactory margin of profit. When, however, your public lands shall have been all conveyed to private hands, at which time the price of land products will not be governed as now by the willingness of labor to make out of their production a mere exchange for fair wages, then, and not till then, will you find capital embarking to any great extent into the business of agriculture.

When this time arrives, a change in your economy will gradually take place. The relations held by labor with capital, which have heretofore been so modified by the easier conditions of the former, with its abundance of free soil to absorb its surplus, will be driven back to its old state of greater dependence. It will no longer experience the great advantage it has held so long in its partnership with the fertile earth. Its depression will reduce the earnings of innumerable monopoly schemes, and the speculative opportunities of capital in the former rapid rise of land values will be reduced to a minimum. The acquirement of land for use and cultivation will then become one of the most promising investments for capital extant. There will be a rise in the price of food staples, and rent for the first time in your history will enter into them as an element of cost.

More than one easily recognized agency of your civilization will tend to reduce the number of your small farms, and to throw the business of food supply completely under the control of your wealthy and capital class. Your small holders now occupying lands of the lower grades of fertility, and who with their limited means but little more than sustain themselves, will readily submit their titles to capitalists, who with the advantage of costly labor saving machines, will find the cultivation of a number of such tracts thrown into one of sufficient profit to engage their means.

The labor saving contrivances which your ingenuity has devised for agricultural pursuits will hasten the demand for larger holdings, and although they greatly cheapen the expense of production, they will not lower the market price of food. While machinery more than makes up for its curtailment of the services of labor, by its cheaper supplies to it in articles of manufacture, no such open and unrestricted competition can exist in the supply of commodities which require, as a necessity of their production, a natural agent whose possession is in every sense of the word a monopoly.

Machinery has never cheapened the supply of raw materials which come directly from the soil, because its use for cultivation has only been exceptional, and it can never become general so long as land is held in small tracts.   This very condition is the one which will engage the attention of investors in land for the profits of use, and at the first permanent advance in the price of your food staples the operation of turning small farms into large ones will begin.

The privilege and the hope of all to get possession of a large or small portion of the earth's surface, gives to your personal ownership system an appearance of fairness not at variance with your popular aspirations of equality, and the evil will not be generally admitted, until it gets to be more seriously felt.

I am sorry to say of you that the principle of equality, as we understand it, has never been sincerely considered or acted upon by any of the governments of the earth.   You have taken it for granted that a serving and dependent class, composing four-fifths of your numbers, must always assist to make up the sum of your population, and no legislative measure can be found in your records which sustains this large body of your people against the encroachments with which wealth and capital are continually permitted to invade their interests.   Liberty itself is of but little value, when life becomes a forfeiture of all the ways and means to improve it. There is, in fact, no liberty in the correct sense,

where all the moments of life must be bartered for
the means to live.

So far as your development has progressed, the
sentiment of brotherhood, as we know it, has never
intruded itself into the spirit of your legislation.
The spectacle of four-fifths of your number toiling
from sun to sun to no purpose but that the balance
may be enriched has inspired no compassion, and
evoked no measure of relief. In the regions of your
authority, where there should be some touch of the
fraternal instinct, nothing presides but the selfish
and mercenary genius of Mamnon. The divine impulse for better things is among you, but instead of
laying out its work in the practical affairs of life, it
has been diverted into the channels of your busy
but unfruitful creeds. You wear your religion like
a holiday garment. We have learned to wear ours
as a common garb.

The past is burnt out, with a residue of but little
value except as a warning. The future is not ours,
but of the universe with its hidden and irrevocable
destiny. The present belongs to us, and it is our
creed to be happy in its possession. We could have
sown fears as you have, and could have been as
overwhelmed with their multiplied terrors. We
could have invented a circumstantial paradise like
yours, with its pathway of extinguished temporal
hopes, and its discouragements of the noblest ambi-

5

tions to build out of the materials in sight; but to what purpose except an unworthy one? The present is ours. Our field is among the living things which surround us. The most of life to us is its possibilities of happiness.

CHAPTER XII.

You must have suspected before this that, so far as the rapid accumulation of wealth is concerned, our society was in that stationary condition so much dreaded by your economists as the end of all material progress. An assumption among your thinkers that only permanent diminishment of the production of wealth is the forerunner of disaster to society, is one of those mistakes easily accounted for by the surroundings of your present stage of development. Your experience teaches you that where the wealth producing energies are in the highest stage of action, your civilization shows all its other forces equally advancing ; and where on the other hand, capital and wealth are restricted, there is a state of general stagnation. These opposite conditions, however, you will find to be, more than anything else, the result of difference in degrees of intelligence, knowledge, and consequently ambition. Your aims, even the higher ones, are so indissolubly connected with wealth as the means by which most of them are promoted, that your incentives to acquire riches have become a part of your intellectual constitution. Where the penalty of a straightened financial condition is the forfeiture of everything which makes life desirable, even a denial of the opportunities of association with the better class, and a surrender of offspring to the degradation and contempt which comes of limited knowledge, it may reasonably be expected that the struggle for wealth would be keen.   Equally as an incentive also are the innumerable avenues of gain, which are everywhere open for the investment of capital, and the remarkable profits which accrue to keep up the spirit of money-making adventure.   You will certainly agree with me that this crushing, elbowing, and treading on each other's heels in the attempt to get money is not the best possible form or type of society : more especially since you are not all fairly and evenly equipped in this struggle, the mass of your people reap no benefit from it, and its result is only to double up the incomes of a few.

Stagnation is not necessarily a condition of the stationary state, as many of your writers lead you to believe.   It is merely a revolution in the aims of society, brought about by changes which are inevitable, and which your civilization is sooner or later bound to reach.   Every newly applied science and invention, and above all every acre of land brought under cultivation, render this period so much dreaded by you more remote ; but you will come to it all the same.   It will merely be a using up of all the resources of capital to *rapidly* multiply itself.   During your present progressive period, so far as that term is applicable to the speedy gathering in of wealth, your society presents to us an aspect of mercenary abandonment beyond anything we have ever experienced ourselves, and with a full knowledge of the end that will come we look forward with a high degree of interest to that time when you will arrive at the stationary condition.

As you approach that period where the diminished profits of capital will discourage the great activity and aggressiveness which now characterize it, some very great changes will gradually be brought about. Assuming that labor will continue to enlighten itself, it will slowly change its relations with capital, so that in the end instead of being below, as it is now, it will be on top, as with us. Many of the ways by which wealth now multiplies itself will be shut off, and with its acquirement no longer indispensable to the honors of life, and the difficulties of its attainment in any large volume increased, society will not be given so intensely to its individual accumulation. Your intellectual activities will be turned more in the direction of other motives. To repair waste and provide for the necessities of the living will be about all that is left to employ your industries, and there will be enough for capital to do within these limits to moderately enlarge itself; while yet within this narrowed field, limited wealth will be able to provide itself with income enough to sustain and reward habits of prudential saving. Although great wealth will be exceedingly difficult to obtain, a fair competency will be within the reach of all ; since labor coming to the front, owing to the weakened powers of wealth, will assume its deserving place in the forces of economy and legislation, and will demand and receive a fairer share of the profits of industry.

After the advance of civilization and knowledge beyond a certain period, the ambitions and necessities of a people will furnish abundant incentives to keep society in a state of activity. The energies of life are stimulated, not so much by the large occasional rewards which come to a few, like prizes in a lottery, as the steady and certain remuneration of each day's output of action to all. The ability to obtain from industry a considerable margin beyond the daily expenses of life is sufficient to keep alive the mental and physical energies, and is certain to bring about that general state of hopefulness, which more than anything else promotes thrift and stimulates ambition.

It may be somewhat at variance with your views of political economy, to believe that any reduction of the power and value of capital will not in a corresponding degree depress labor. You must bear in mind, however, that the stationary state, as exemplified by our society, differs from your progressive condition, not in the lesser abundance of capital, but in its better diffusion, more dependent relations, and smaller comparative profits. It follows from this as a matter of course, that it requires the possession of a larger amount of the products of labor to bring about that condition of life known as a competency than it does with you. But by a well determined arrangement in all ways in favor of those who toil, by which a fair margin is secured between income and expense, the coveted independence is always within reach.

Under our system, capital becoming diffused among the masses in comparatively small portions, and having no such extraordinary uses, nor such high rates of interest as with you, it assumes its natural place as an adjunct to all the enterprises of labor. All our factories are consequently carried on by co-operation. No such a thing is known on our planet as the owner of a manufacturing establishment depressing at his will and pleasure the pay of perhaps a whole community of working people. When an establishment is required for the manufacture of some product in demand, our workmen undertake it as a business belonging wholly to themselves, and there is never any lack of means among them to do it.

The utterly helpless condition of your workmen,

as a class, is not entirely owing to their enforced scant share in the profits of industry. Whoever among them, by greater abstinence or otherwise, succeeds in saving any considerable portion of his earnings, hastens either to change his situation for that of employer, where self-interest inclines him to favor low wages, or to seek among the greater encouragements outside a change of occupation. By this process capital and labor are constantly being divorced, and the ranks of your workmen are left to contain only those whose necessities hold them there.

In the condition of things with us, bestowing upon labor all the emoluments of industry, it becomes the most advantageous pursuit of life. With wages at a uniform and fixed sum, from which there can be no deviation except to increase, the working man proceeds to lay by his surplus, until, in a reasonable time, it can be made to do service in adding to the fruits of his toil.

In our society there is no possibility, and no one has hopes of gaining money by chance. We hold it to be a demoralizing evil that wealth should be obtained without industry. The quality of mind which you honor under the name of shrewdness, and which seldom hesitates to profit by the losses and even the miseries of others, would find life a burden on account of the odium attached, in

any community on our planet. The privilege to
build up an individual fortune, by taking from the
substance of the whole people in any unlimited degree which an unscrupulous ingenuity can devise, is
one of the peculiarities of your civilization. To this
general license, with its very small limitation, is to
be ascribed most of your social miseries. The lessons presented to your youth at the very first glance
at the affairs of life are calculated to impress them
with the belief that success is not so much for the
strong and considerate, as it is for the wary and cunning ; and that the business of creating wealth is of
the slightest importance, when compared with the
many successful arts and schemes for capturing it
after its production. The example is witnessed
everywhere among you, of money-making without
loss of honor or respect, by the method of drawing
from others, by taking advantage of their necessities,
excessive and unfair portions of their substance for
some sort of service rendered. The consequence
is that life with you is constantly renewed, on the
one hand, by persons with more or less inherited capital, who are educated to believe that existence is a
game, whose winning instances are the best guides
to follow ; and on the other by the great mass of her-
editary toilers who submit themselves as victims under sheer force of necessity and usage. This state
of your civilization brings into play many of your

lower feelings, as indispensable instruments of success. When selfishness is the chief promoter of thrift,
practical charity is only aroused by unusual provo-
cation.   The miseries of existence are unseen and
unfelt by others than the sufferers themselves among
you, just as your senses become oblivious to the presence of disturbing influences which you find it un-
profitable to suppress.   The necessity for each one
looking out for himself in your fierce battles of life
makes him unmindful of others.   Yet benevolence
dwells within all your hearts as a divine attribute,
which cannot be wholly destroyed, no matter how
neglected its cultivation. Like the retarded germin-
ation of seed in a too deeply surmounting soil, it
comes to the light among you here and there, under
favorable conditions, with an increasing frequency
which reveals your destiny as unerringly as the gold-
en horizon presages the coming of the sun.

The difference in the degree by which each individual holds the common welfare in comparison with
his own, marks the stage of progress towards perfection in society.   You hold within yourselves, by
a divine provision, the elements to this end.   Your
history is full of instances to prove that self-sacrifice
is an act which inspires a greater commendation
than any other.   All your normal mental organizations are endowed with the propensity to benefit others, which only the conditions of your society cir-

cumscribe by a conflict of interest. What is now in
your higher faculties, during your present development, a pleasure, will become a passion by further
progress and cultivation, and, by a still more extended pursuit, a necessity to the tranquility and enjoyment of your lives. Filial and parental love from
mere instincts have grown among you to be the most
gratifying of inclinations. Sexual affinity, from its
origin of brutal desire, has been transformed, in your
higher circles, to a pure and tender sentiment of dis-
interested regard. Not long ago your lunatics were
chained to stakes like beasts. Your infected were
left to die upon the roadsides. Your infirm were
shut from sight, consumed with vermin among
their rags. You house, clothe, and care for all these
now with almost the solicitude that parents bestow
upon children. If you should submit yourselves now
for a time to the presence of these old inhumanities,
and observe their disturbing effects upon the happiness of your lives, it would be a fair measurement of
your progress toward the stationary state.

Supposing yourself to be one of an audience as-
sembled for the purpose of obtaining pleasure from
a performance on the stage, your delight would, in
a large degree, depend upon the manifestations of
approval surrounding you. Any expression of dis-
satisfaction would spoil your enjoyment, no matter
upon what it might be founded. It might arise, for

instance, from unfair opportunities of view, or from the usurped privilege of some to obstruct the vision of others. Your inclinations, arising from no higher motive than self interest, would lead you to assist in bringing about that state of general satisfaction which is indispensable to your own comfort and happiness. This illustrates one of the motives which, in our stage of development, impels us to arrange that, so far as possible, every individual shall enjoy equal privileges in society. Happiness is simply not possible without it.

Your moralists might argue that too close and intimate a sympathy with the misfortunes of others would keep us so constantly unhappy as to make life unendurable. In answer to this, you have only to consider that if you separate from all your ills those which either directly or remotely are brought upon you by your imperfect social state, there are but few left besides death and its attendant sorrows. And of these few entirely comprised under the heads of sickness and accidents, there is a possibility of their greater diminishment by better modes of life.

That you are slowly and gradually moving towards the stationary condition, unmistakable evidence proves. Material as well as spiritual indications confirm this belief. You can easily observe that wealth in the hands of the few is losing its opportunities for rapid increase. In your oldest

advanced regions it has already worked out its resources to the extent of endeavoring to find abroad
occasions for profitable use. But for the monopoly
of land, which enables it to extract from industry
an amount for its services out of all proportion with
its value elsewhere, it would have been much further advanced towards this stationary state.

One of the greatest obstacles opposing your approach towards the perfect society is your propensity
to theorize and speculate upon matters which it is
not given you to know. We have a saying that he
who gets his feet in the air is lost. We mean by
that to convey the idea, that all speculation not
founded on positive knowledge is so utterly worth-
less, that any indulgence therein is useless to society. The opinion is unchallenged among us, that
the inhabitants of the Earth are too prone to get their
feet in the air. And yet the very ease by which
this misfortune is accomplished among you is a proof
of your goodness. Your inclination to virtue is your
weak side of approach, and all your inherent and
intuitive charity, which might during all these centuries have been exercised upon yourselves, has
been to a great extent wasted upon your schemes of
salvation, in which you have no assurance whatever
but the wild promises of imagination. When you
come fully to understand that happiness, true prosperity, virtue, and even beauty are but synonyms

of truth, and that misery, crime, misfortune, and ugliness are but other names for falsehood, you will no longer have any dread or hesitation to search for that verity which destroys old beliefs, even though that search melts into air your most cherished traditions. You will come to understand after a while that a truth can disseminate nothing but good ; and that a falsehood, no matter how venerable with age, nor how respectable by adoption, can generate little else than evil. Your creeds have attracted you and plowed deep into your affections, because in them is gathered from yourselves the divine sentiments of goodness, out of which they are all robed in a pretended monopoly. Your virtues are brought into service within their narrow limits, and your energies and substance consumed in the work of enlarging their influence, while the more fruitful material for your charities lies neglected in the evils and miseries of your society.

The Earth is your dominion. Tread firmly upon it. Remember it has been put into your keeping, and that your people are entirely responsible for its social condition. He who assists to improve that, serves the Deity better than he who spends his life in genuflections and prayers. When you look around among the wretched criminals among you, punished and unpunished, and the poverty-stricken, and the sad-eyed, neglected children ; see the unsuppressed temptations to evil, the unrecognized virtue, and the uneven opportunities for individual advancement, you should bear in mind that all these are but evidences of the violation of the trust imposed in you by the divine intelligence. · There is, perhaps, no spectacle upon the Earth that inspires more pity among the inhabitants of Mars, than the constant waste of your best parts in submitting yourselves to the impositions of your seers, who lead you away from your duties, under the theory that the Earth is merely a battle ground and field of conquest for the perpetuation of their doctrines, all else upon it being blank vanities. They have kept you away from the true business of your lives, and have mesmerized you, alternately terrifying and delighting you by unreal fancies ; now exhibiting to you a paradise and at another time a nightmare. They have involved you in a perpetual shadow, discouraging you of all hopes of brightness until your celestial birth. By exhibiting only your grosser parts, and threatening the vengeance of an austere and capricious god of their own imaginary creation, they both degrade you and belittle your conceptions of the Deity. You could bend your faces upward with a better sincerity, if, instead of following phantoms all these ages, with your feet in the air, you could show a truer interpretation of the divine purpose in establishing a happier and more perfect dwelling together.

CHAPTER XIII.

I RESIDE within a city of Mars which, in point of
population and grandeur, is one of the first on our
planet. In accordance with our custom of desig-
nating such places with names of quality, it would
be known in your language as the city of Good
Will. As it is the type of all others, you are already
informed of a few of its general features. I will,
however, give you some further description of our
society and surroundings, in only the hasty and imperfect manner which this opportunity affords.

With much the same feelings and inclinations as
yours, and with that love and cultivation of the
beautiful which we have pursued as an element of
our religion, uninterrupted as with you by those
delusions which destroys art, we have advanced
much beyond you in that direction.

It is to be noted, as a coincidence proving the
unity of all intelligence within the universe, that
we have designed an architecture not unlike that of
your ancient Greece. Our isolated exteriors, such
as villas and country residences, bear a close re-
semblance to some of your ancient styles. In our
cities we have been obliged to conform to the condition of aerial navigation, which has greatly re-

stricted our elevated ornamentation, and forced
upon us a system of curves instead of angles in our
projections.

One of the most notable differences between your
construction and ours is the material and form of
our roofs, which are uniformly of solid glass, and
dome shaped. The substance is laid on in a plastic
state, hardens in a short time, is purely transparent,
and as difficult to fracture as stone. The upper
story of every house becomes by this method the
chief source of light for its interior, and by ingeniously formed horizontal curtains can be darkened
at will. We believe this to be one of the most important sanitary arrangements we possess, and to
which may be chiefly ascribed the health and vigor
of our bodies. In these bright upper apartments we
bathe ourselves in the sun, and enjoy the constant
bloom and fragrance of flowers.

By a natural adaptation, these glass roofs have
become inseparably connected with our religious
lives. Our interest in the wonderful nightly exhibitions which they permit is increased by the general knowledge we have cultivated of the character
and motions of the heavenly bodies. As a consequence, there are but few among us who cannot describe the paths and directions of the planets; and it
is quite safe to say that a majority of our people can
compute the periods of opposition and conjunction

between them.   No other exhibition so feeds and
stimulates our religious impulses, as the grand dis-
play of divine power in the unceasing motions of
the spheres.   We bring the spectacle within our
households, and dwell with it.   It is the altar upon
which we worship the great unseen.

Each block of buildings is surmounted by a single
roof of the transparent character I have described.
In this way we have utilized all the space for dwelling or business purposes, and prevented those un-
sightly back yards which disfigure the cities of the
Earth and lower their sanitary condition.   Usually
there are no partition walls except in the lower
stories, and these lofty upper apartments, especially
if over dwellings, have their flattened dome-shaped
roofs supported by a series of columns and arches
artistically wrought and decorated, and their inte-
riors adorned with growing flowers and statuary, so
as to furnish a delightful resort, convenient to the
neighborhood and open to all.

These extensive halls are a necessity to the social
character of our people.   You may imagine how an
intercourse based on perfect equality, and with the
paramount idea of obtaining pleasure by bestowing
it, would have its enjoyments enlarged by the unrestricted and unselected numbers participating. Music
and dancing are delights with us beyond your experience.   We enjoy the advantages of atmospheric

conditions and a degree of gravitating force which
are peculiarly adapted to heighten these enjoyments.
Our voice tones, seldom without cultivation, acquire
an energy and brilliancy in our atmosphere unknown
to you. A combination of trained voices with us is
so vastly superior to instrumental music, that the
latter is not known except as a novelty. Since the
force of gravity is less with us our bodies are much
lighter than yours, and our motions are consequently more airy and graceful. In movements like dancing there is less muscular energy expended, and a
greater pleasure attained.

Under these vast transparent domes, looking out
upon the universe of planets and stars, we dance,
and sing our hymns of praise to the Deity, asking
for nothing, but uniting our voices in the rhythms
of poetry and music in a thanksgiving for the pleasures of life, and for that guidance which has directed
us clear of the deadly superstitions of our neighboring planet, and for that intelligence which has led
us to find our true religious duties in exercising our
better impulses within our own fields of action.

Over our business quarters these upper stories,
less ornate and well ventilated, serve the purposes
of factories and work shops, where the sun's rays,
not so intense as with you, owing to our greater
distance from it, are let in to brighten the hours of
those who toil. Among these locations of industry

are conditions that would surprise you. There is
the indispensable anteroom beside the entrance of
each, where, enjoying the comfortable furniture,
may be found a number of operatives waiting for
the beginning of the three-hour shift. They are all
on terms of easy familiarity, yet among them may
be found the president of the grand council, who
manages the affairs of the city, the lecturer who
presides at the temple, and other prominent worthies
mingled with the others who have achieved no honors beyond the work bench. The person who is
most complimented among the number is the one
who has just been granted an advance of one grade
in the skill of his calling. He has attained what
would be an equivalent in your society to the honors
of a collegiate degree, with the very material difference in his favor, that for years to come, and perhaps
as long as he lives, his income is permanently increased by an enhanced value to his labor. No competition will ever, under our system, render value-
less this achievement of his.

Your degrees of learning are but empty honors
compared with this profitable distinction. You in-
sure no certain rewards for that acquirement of
knowledge which has won its parchment of approval, and the holder enjoys only the slim advantage
which his certificate secures. His degree wins him
no bread, and the honors of his career rest uncertain.

with all his struggles ahead. Our workman, at each step of his advancement, increases his income, under the assurance and protection of our industrial methods, with the certainty and stability of a government pension.

But while we have found it wise to honor and protect manual skill, the physical strength of our people has for many ages been a subject of general attention. Among the productions of the supreme author which he is engaged in perfecting and beautifying, the first in importance on your planet is surely man himself, as a being animal as well as mental. As an indolent, weak and passive body is usually associated with a mind of the same character, it is only by the cultivation of both together that society improves. You have evidences enough of the inseparable connection between mental and physical energy, and yet your cultivation of the body has engaged but little attention. It seems to us one of the most serious objections to your religious abstractions, that the spirit of all of them tends to deny or belittle the great service of healthy sinews and nerves in the progress of social improvement.

You will find intellectual stagnation everywhere upon the face of the Earth, where incentives to muscular action are suppressed from whatever cause, and you know by experience that the decay of mental vigor, by a release from the necessity of bodily exercise, has obliged the brawn and muscle of your age, iu more than one instance, to come to the front in the management of affairs.

Civilization, at a certain degree of its progress, is expected to assume duties which, until then, have been faithfully performed by nature alone. Like a good mother she has provided, in your primitive state, against the degeneration of your bodies by the operation of her universal law, the survival of the fittest. In your social betterment you can reasonably be expected to provide for yourselves some substitute to maintain that standard of hardihood and strength which had formerly been kept up by your primitive struggles for existence.

Your knowledge of the laws of heredity has enabled you to improve upon the forms and qualities of all those creatures which have been taken from their native wilds to serve your uses ; and yet, with a fatal inconsistency, you consign your own bodies to a carelessness of procreation which totally ignores all well known methods of improvement. The spectacle is common among you, of the skilled breeder straining his knowledge to remedy defects of form in the lower animals in his possession, while he and his progeny exhibit, in their own bodies, without concern or attention, the very same physical infirmities which he had so sucessfully banished in his brutes by parental selection.

The neglect of your opportunities in this direction is more surprising, when it is considered how greatly you are suffering from it ; for although the achievement of a more general perfection of form and strength is invaluable to you, as laying the foundation of a larger average of mental power and activity, yet this is not more important to your society than the easy and certain eradication by judicious matings of the most persistent and fatal of your diseases. It is appaling to estimate the sum of human misery perpetually transmitted congenitally in diseased tissues and functional defects.

This evil, which has prevailed among you until your bodily ills are almost innumerable, you have been taught to consider as an arrangement of the divine will, and you rest yourselves helplessly in the belief that its endurance without remedy is the penalty of life ; when, in fact, it is perpetuated chiefly by that over-powering individual selfishness which makes no account of the general good while gratifying sentiments of feeling, pleasure, or greed.

I have already drawn your observation to that infallible test which marks the progress of social development—the average willingness of attention and sacrifice of individual interests to the common welfare. From our achievements in that direction already described, you may easily imagine that we have not neglected the opportunity to improve and benefit society by the observance of some of nature's simplest and most easily applied laws.

We are not embarrassed as you would be by protests of an infringement of personal liberty, because we have arrived beyond that stage where law and its enforcement are required. Official recommendation, supported by a united public opinion, without any penalty for non-compliance except the general condemnation, is our only resort in directing the conduct of our people. Under such a system, any violation of individual rights is impossible. It is enough in our society to determine that a measure is for the common good, to secure its adoption without dissent.

Accordingly, it comes within the province of our Government Health Department to direct, and in some degrees supervise, those marital engagements out of which our numbers are so constantly replenished. This important business is closely associated with measures designed in other ways to promote our health, and may be said to begin at the birth of every child. Each infant is carefully examined by medical experts, and registered. Every peculiarity or bodily defect is recorded, and rules of management furnished, as remedies, if found necessary. Every person, young or old, is required periodically to pass a like examination. The personal health register is open to all, and the bodily condition of every inhabitant may be in that way ascertained. None fail to avail themselves of information so greatly concerning themselves. Incipient diseases are in a vast number of cases remedied by this discovery of their unsuspected presence, and the habits of life are often changed in time to head off some latent malady, which, in its early stages, nothing but medical science could reveal.

This system establishes a public record of the physical standing, either in lurking disease or deformity, of every individual; and as it is made the duty of our health department to declare its judgment of approval in every marriage contract, we have no transmitted diseases or deformities of body running through generations, and multiplying the miseries of life, as you have. We have long ago stamped out by this method three-fourths of the diseases which are nourished by the habits of civilization. By this means we have secured a race of men and women so physically perfect as to cause existence to be accepted as a grateful patrimony. You have interrogated nature in her laws of development, and in her processes of modification both in forms and qualities of things, and with a knowledge so acquired, you have cultivated a world of animal and vegetable organisms to your better service. We have done that, too; but we have accomplished in that line something of incomparably more importance to us, in advancing together by due cultivation and care our animal as well as our intellectual selves.

You cannot fail to discover in this, one of the effects of that striking divergence between our civilization and yours, due to widely different interpretations of the divine will. We look upon our planet with all its appurtenances as a bequest which has been delivered into our keeping for that assistance in progression so plainly the best and most exalted business of our lives, and so unmistakably pleasing to the supreme author that every degree of its accomplishment is rewarded by signs of his favor. From our better demonstrated spiritual belief, we derive the inspiration to increase and bestow upon each other the best things of life ; while you, under religious promptings from the same high source, condemn yourselves to abstinence and austerity. You so misconceive the true relations between spiritual and material forces, that instead of regarding each as the nursery and builder-up of the other, you have devised a theory which brings them into antagonism as diverse influences ; the exercise of material concerns, as you assume, tending to lead you away from the divinity.

The effect of this mistaken view of life is plainly to be seen in your society and surroundings. Your material progression, deprived of the religious im-

pulse and enthusiasm, and depending wholly upon
the lower faculty of self-gain, advances by slow degrees, frequently retrogresses, and is not secure of a
total relapse under so mercenary a moving power.
Your forward movement, instead of being compact
and co-operative like ours, drags along fitfully and
laboriously, marshaled alone by the struggling influence here and there, under the dead weight of
an indifferent and self absorbed multitude, and in
open conflict with a host of disturbed traditions.

Your doctrine of the absolute divorce of spiritual
and material interests, by wasting your best parts
in the service of the world-condemning deity of your
imagination, and by surrendering your temporal
affairs to the sole exercise of your lower sentiments
and feelings, has spread its dire effects, and may be
traced in every phase of your society. Out of it comes
that singular disregard for each other in all things
except the spiritual, and that perverted estimate of
goodness, which has consigned your science and
learning with their influences, together with your
whole world of industry, to places where unassisted
and unencouraged they must work out their own
doubtfully admitted and tardy rewards ; while your
best enthusiasm and most active morality is led to
waste among your many unreasoning schemes of salvation.

What but this unwarranted dissociation of spirit

and matter, of the body and soul, of your physical and intellectual parts, regarding one as the de-
grading yokemate of the other instead of its counterpart and co-worker, has taken all the heart out of
your lives, hidden from you the moral possibilities
within your worldly reach, and reduced the only
existence you are so far called upon to improve into
a dead and useless hibernation of your divinest faculties? What more readily excuses and defends
your indifference to the hard lines of human labor,
and your toleration of a system which dooms most
of you to perpetual dependence, than those moss-
grown traditions which, from their selected quarters
among the supernatural and unseen, are not disturbed
or interested by your social wrongs, and which in
truth find their best patronage and most profitable
employment where most prevail the miseries of life?
Just in the degree in which you are already emanci-
pated from these barren illusions, does your most
humane work in social progress appear.

Your inspirations of goodness come to you as they
come to us, without the necessity of a revelation.
Their encouragement is more faithfully secured by
the benign influence which rewards their adoption,
than those written codes among you which assume,
under doubtful motives, their direction and control.
As surely as all the forces of nature may be traced
to the heat of the sun, so your impulses of virtue,

your heroism of good deeds, and your spiritual hopes, are conveyed to you in a germinal state without any intercepting medium, with the first breath of your bodies ; to be improved, enlarged and harvested for the purposes and uses of your society.

You turn over the surface of the Earth and gather its fruits, never doubting the superhuman forces in conjunction which reward your labor ; and yet your intellectual tillage is left to take its chances among circumscribed opportunities which no combined effort has attempted to enlarge. Your progress cannot be otherwise than uncertain and slow, and your governments will always be unstable in their foundations under your system, which at its best furnishes scarcely one disciplined mind in a hundred, and the acquirements of that one, too, resulting only from a spontaneous individual impulse, with, in most cases, no higher motives than self-gain and advancement.

Your fields are not wanting in your attentions. You bring profit to yourselves by the thorough tillage of your acres. You multiply by your manipulation under nature's hints the life-supporting and pleasure-giving properties of the fruits and flowers of the Earth to the extremest blossoming and abundance. And yet in such a state of fallow is your own divine essence of reason and thought, that to this day no superstition is too absurd, no sophistry too transparent, and no pretended reform too ill digested to take root and flourish, even to the disintegration of large patches of your social life. So that while no fault can be found with your progress in the handling of the material agents under your control, the opinion is irresistible, from our point of view, that you are assiduously cultivating everything but yourselves.

CHAPTER XIV.

WE have, like you, wealth with its self-rewarding luxuries, but its character is very different. Its chosen pleasures and inclinations are unlike yours. Acquisitiveness has no such controlling motives as with you. The hope of social elevation, the anxiety to place the sufferings of poverty beyond reach, and the love of power, are not elements in our desire for gain. As an inducement to the accumulation of wealth, all these motives are supplanted by the one overweening passion for distinguishment which its possession affords, by contributing to the well-being and happiness of others. The even opportunities of life, and the entire absence of poverty as you have it, with its miseries, do away with the most fertile stimulus to individual greed among you; and the strong passion to hoard, which you call avarice, becomes with us, from the singleness of its motives, one of the noblest of our religious aspirations. Whatever luxuries wealth provides for itself are shared by all; and since the nature and form of our society precludes the necessity of alms-giving, charity, as you understand it, is unknown. The general dissemination of self-pride and independence, as much the result of our religious beliefs as of our political and educational methods, secures us against those evils of indiscriminate charity which are found to paralyze industry everywhere upon the Earth, in its present stage of development.

In our political system we have provided so well for the even and sufficient reward of toil, that our animal requirements, so easily supplied, are never wanting in individual cases to the extent of suffering. In the extremity of invalidism or other misfortune, assistance comes, not in the form of charity as you know it, but as the anxious and sympathetic support of a family to one of its members in distress. The field of benevolence in wealth is, therefore, entirely within the province of education and art; which, in accordance with our religious aspirations and beliefs, takes the same form in their furtherance of the purposes of the Deity as your devotional enterprises of promulgating your religious faiths.

Our rich contribute largely from their substance to the purposes of education, with a philanthropy that is greatly intensified by the religious enthusiasm gratified by the act; but they do not build nor contribute to our temples of worship as yours do, since the attendance upon these is unsolicited and voluntary, and a mere pleasurable gratification of our spiritual hopes and aspirations. Unattended by saving forms and conditions, as with you, the worship within our temples is not considered of consequence to our spiritual welfare. These religious centers, unlike yours, assume no power to condone or compromise with evil. No burdened, unclean conscience comes to them with the hope of absolution, to return again laden with its misdeeds for another purging. No wholesale peculator brings a portion of his evil gains as an atonement for the inflicted miseries of his avaricious career. There is nothing whatever within our temples or surrounding them, but the peace and self conscious satisfaction of the divine coöperation in our efforts to cultivate ourselves, and the praise and glory of our own success forms the spirit of our worship.

Our society being without exclusiveness, and the ostentation of riches a thing unknown, there is no ambition to get beyond the general fare in dwellings. The whole city block, surmounted by its one continuous roof, may be either a single or a number of dwellings, to accord with the incomes of its occupants. Under our land system the cost of rent is such a small item in the living expenses, that all are enabled to share alike in their housings, and to equally enjoy the benefit of our wholesome sanitary provisions. No one amongst us dwells in a hovel. We labor that the surroundings of all shall be uniformly pleasant and comfortable. With us the suspicion of unseen misery is enough to disturb the pleasures of life. Besides the unpleasant suggestions of discomfort which a rough and incommodious dwelling would arouse, it would be considered by us a painful violation of taste, and a sacrifice of the opportunities of art.

Consequently, within the limits of our cities you will not find any external distinction among our dwelling places, to denote the financial standing of their occupants. But as a whole block becomes occasionally occupied by a single family, whose large fortune enables them to enjoy its magnificent proportions, there is not wanting within those luxuries of wealth urged by the prevailing tastes. The establishment becomes the pride and pleasure of its locality. In conformity with all other of the city's blocks, it has three lofty stories. The lower one on each of its façades consists of a series of Corinthian columns with highly wrought capitals, resting upon which, and forming the second story elevation, are a line of arches, supporting the flush outer walls of the story above. This story, which is abundantly lighted by its transparent roof, has its exterior surface decorated in bas relief with architraves and cornices designed in our elaborate styles. Every block has an arched and vestibuled main entrance at each of its four corners, over which there rises a tower containing a powerful electric light, illuminating at night the interior as well as the surrounding streets. As our thoroughfares which radiate from the city's cen-

ter are straight, and better adapted for business and
the industries, they are devoted to these purposes.
Consequently, on the circular or concentric streets
are located most of our dwellings; the choicest of
which, as to location, are those fronting the parks,
which, as I have already given you to understand,
circumscribe at intervals every neighborhood of the
city.   It is, then, in these convex or concave fronts,
standing on opposite lines of the park belt, that the
abodes of wealth are mostly to be found.

You would discover the whole of one of these
buildings, except its middle story, devoted to the
use of the public, and containing on its first floor a
number of class rooms assigned to a system of teaching to which your kindergartens bear some similar-
ity, and a few others in which the scholars have
advanced to a higher grade.   The character of the
instruction would be indicated by the appliances and
implements of industry everywhere to be seen, the
busy use of them at intervals by the classes, and
the pride and emulation of the scholars, in their
struggling efforts towards skill in their handling.
In another room you would find a smaller class, the
special proteges of the owner, composed of a few,
who, by the early manifestations of unusual promise,
were being assisted in their pursuance of some
branch of science or art.

Outside of this department of instruction you

would find an extensive library, with its reading room attachments ingeniously arranged for convenience, and a large apartment, usually in the center of the building, well lighted from the roof, in which was collected the art treasures, and upon which was lavished by its owner that fondness for the beautiful which becomes him as a member of our society.

The upper story is a public assembly chamber for occasions of rejoicing and pleasure, and is adorned with statuary, fountains, and blooming plants. This grand apartment is so tempered in warmth by the cheap appliances of our municipality, that it becomes a winter garden during our long, inclement seasons, when the parks are sere and icy.

One of these establishments would suggest to your view an exaggerated estimate of its founder's wealth. In most cases his income extends but little beyond the support of this enterprise. In his dream of wealth he has achieved the hope of his ambition, and he stops there.

Your passion of hoarding beyond a competency, without purpose except the lust of hoarding, is the offshoot of that instinct in the carnivorous brute, which impels him to refuse to his hungry fellows any portion of his captured carcass, one-tenth of which he cannot consume. This low and brute-born heritage of greed only fails of a better suppression in your society, because you have neglected to en-

tirely remedy, by your political methods, the generally precarious way in which your animal and intellectual wants are supplied. Suffering now follows
just as close to a miss in your struggles for sustenance, as it did when your skin-clad hunters failed of
their game.

Your passion to get and hold is intensified and
brutalized in its lack of regard for the consequences
to others, by the large number of artificial necessities only attainable in your society by a considerable accumulation of money, the want of which
implies degradation, and a sacrifice of many things
that have grown to be dear to life. Every addition
to the savings removes to a greater distance that
dreaded condition of your civilization, known as
poverty. The insatiable character of the hoarding
is not unlike the motive of overcaution in a wan-
derer, who, terrorized by the appearance of a dreaded animal in his path, increases his distance by flight
far beyond all possible approach of the dangerous
presence.

Your breathless pursuit of wealth, beyond all
reasonable limit of obtaining the objects of desire,
is induced also by the remarkable opportunities its
possession affords to appropriate the earnings of industry. The capacity of your wealth to absorb and
control the fruits of toil exists in a geometrical ratio
of increase with the greater wealth employed, and

the taste of power once felt is seldom appeased, but increases with every money addition. Under your favorable laws, it may extend to the privilege of a single individual exacting the whole surplus earnings of an army of busy workers.

Through centuries of legislation and usage you have established various processes, by which wealth is enabled to extract an undue portion of the earnings of industry. Among these processes may be named rates of interest on money graded to the necessities of borrowers, rents gauged by the ability of tenants to pay, monopoly supplies with prices fixed just below the point of compelled abstinence, variations in the value of mediums of exchange, with other unsuppressed agencies promoting frequent change of values for the opportunities of capital and the distress of labor ; stupendous aggregations of wealth reversing the laws of economy by advancing the price of necessities on the one hand and depressing the wages of labor on the other ; and more successful than all, a system of land proprietorship which permits holders of the Earth's surface, in addition to their privilege of exacting a large portion of the profits of industry in rent, a further right to pocket, in the form of appreciated values of their land, an unearned share of the collective fruits of the industries which surround them.

Our divergent views of existence are exemplified

in the care we have taken to provide for an evener
division of the products of industry. With us, property is the means, and not the end, beyond which
there are any number of attainments in life incomparably more desirable and beneficial to society, and
our legislation has been directed chiefly to the care
and cultivation of these. The great aim of our government has been to provide for the well-being of
persons, while it may be said of yours that the most
attention has been devoted to the welfare of property; by which is meant its protection and increase,
regardless of the manner of its distribution, or the
doubtful methods of its extraction from the energies
of labor. In the pursuit of this policy you are only
perpetuating, without much change, your primitive
conditions, when the strong arm gathered the most
of the wealth. Your early born instincts do not
seem sufficiently evolutionized to co-operate in any
undertaking which denies opportunities of the strong
over the weak; and the unhappy consequence is a
society so mercenary that the general estimate
among you is not from any quality which indicates
a nearness to the Deity, but principally from the
cool numerical calculations of property attachments.

The unity of our spiritual and temporal interests
makes it necessary that every government act shall
be a religious one. The spirit of kindness and charity to all which is the only deserving part of your

religions, we have taken as the foundation of all our
public acts, and have made it the cornerstone of
government itself. Our legislation, if the mere assent to measures recommended can be called by that
name, considers first the welfare of persons com-
prising the whole, subservient to which every possible interest must take its place. And the welfare
of persons, in our politico-religious point of view,
is dependent upon the proper and equitable rewards
of industry; their equal opportunities of acquiring
knowledge; an encouragement of their morality by
a recognition of their virtues, making it the necessary stepping-stone to their advancement; and the
sweeping away of every social form which establishes a sense of inferiority, destroys the pride of
self, and institutes that feeling of degradation which
is the most prolific source of evil in society.

It is easy to note your tendency in these directions. The barbaric institution of force and its
concomitant of fear, as agencies in the management
and control of men, is gradually being eliminated
from all your progressive governments, and the better methods of assent and co-operation are getting
in their salutary work of emancipation. Knowledge is spreading itself among you—no longer a
dessert only upon a few favored tables, but a chief
dish under the newly acquired appetites of the
many. The glamour of your wealth and the im-

pressiveness of your religion are losing their rever-
ential respect, with the focused light directed upon
their doubtful origins. You have inaugurated the
beginning of a new faith, with better spiritual foundations, not condemning the world and its society,
but loving it, following in the footsteps of the divine presence within its limits, taking a hand in its
affairs, and directing them towards the better possibilities in view.

Ah, my brother, the coming of your Messiah was
both more and less than you have imagined. The
era of new and better things in social development
is preceded by the gradual decay of old convictions,
which have served their time and are no longer useful, except in their place within the catalogue of
traditions to mark the progress of thought.

Society assumes its beliefs under an impulse of
progression, as much controlled by evolutionary
laws as the organic substances of the Earth. No
one can teach the world. With a free exercise of
its intellectual faculty, it teaches itself. The power
of an idea, among the moral forces, is in its corresponding with a proper stage of development to receive it. A solitary thought is useless, as a moral
agent, without its already existing half-formed fig-
ments scattered about in society. Its power to move
lies in the coalescence of its parts. Ideas 'and beliefs have been adopted at different stages of your

civilization, and have served as great motors to progress, which, ages before, were enunciated without impression. Society rids itself of its rudimentary impressions and beliefs, in much the same manner that an animal, under changing environments, sheds its old organs and develops new ones. Every new belief affecting society is subservient to it, and is only adopted slowly and by degrees. If it be a truth making its way, its final installation is marked by an unquestioned acquiescence and an undisturbed tranquility. If an error, agitation and unrest mark the whole period of its accession.

The coming of your Messiah was more than you have supposed, because grander and more imposing than its assumed supernaturalisms was its enthronement of two central ideas. One was the adoption of the sentiment of brotherhood as a means of adjusting the relations of men with each other, and the other was the inauguration of spiritual hope as a guide in the actions of life. Out of this beginning has come all that is good in your social progress. The general acceptance of these ideas, as agencies in your civilization, began its work by weakening the old society, and it finally destroyed it by extinguishing the bands of physical force which held it together. The cultivation of these inspirational beliefs in their purity, as they were bestowed upon you by the divine intelligence, would have soon brought to you the same peace and good will that they have shed upon the inhabitants of Mars; but you were not to be indulged so soon in this happy offering. The few, who had been dominating the many for ages, appropriating their earnings, and even sacrificing their lives, in a lust for power and wealth, were not to let escape them so fine an opportunity to hold the simple-minded by a new agency, ten-fold more subjugating than the old method of coercion by force. The religious superstition of the age, a mere diversion for the untaught multitude, inert and unpromising, was vitalized by the infusion of these new, humane and spiritual impulses; and, with many added ingeniously contrived supernaturalisms, and an attractive moral code, it was built up into a system and organized into a society which has borne its heavy weight upon your progress, and spread its dominion more successfully than the warlike legions it supplanted. It has accomplished no good which is not entirely due to the irresistible expansion of the truths it appropriated at its inception out of nature's evolutionary process of social development, viz., the regard for one another, as a guide in all the actions of life, and that hope eternal which spiritualizes and elevates our existence.

The coming of your Messiah was less than you have believed, because you have mistaken a person-

ality, in which the genius of advanced and salutary
doctrines manifested itself, for a part and presence
of the Deity himself.   As the promulgation of
thoughts that are conceived under the inspiration
and pressure of a natural force in the process of
social development is less than the awful presence
and verbal communication of the Deity, so, in the
same degree, was the coming of your Messiah less.

But you will have a second coming, my brother,
unperverted by the craft of your seers, and uncon-
taminated with the superstitions of a crude society
like the first.   It will be of you and a part of you,
raising you up to a higher esteem of yourselves,
glorifying you as the progenitors of all good, under
a divine and irresistible law of betterment.   It will
relieve you of the evil thoughts that have con-
demned and degraded you.   The new hope, like a
newly discovered strength, will push out in all directions, in the exercise of its salutary work.   Instead of discourse and exhortation to the lowly and
down trodden, with promises as impossible of denial as of verification, it will lift them upon their
feet by the strong hand of a better social method.
Like the first coming, its symbolic picture will be
carved into monuments, reproduced in all the de-
partments of art, and cherished as the chief re-
minder of your duties and obligations to the Deity.
It will be no symbol of anguish and sorrow, like

the first, but in place of it *the divine figure of a strong man supporting and encouraging a weak one.* Yes, my brother, you will have a s-e-c-o-n-d c-o-m—

WHAT is all this? I raise myself upon my couch. The sun is an hour up. Through my window I see an enquiring group, marvelling at my tardiness. My cows linger for their milking, and utter their complaints in a gentle lowing. My pet deer stand with their large wondering eyes fixed upon me, and the appearance of my face at the pane has drawn toward me my whole restless and scrambling flock of poultry, impatient for their morning feed. I look toward the easy chair and it is empty. My celestial visitor has departed.